# Sweet Valley HIGH®

## Power Play

Sweet Valley HIGH®

Double Love

Secrets

Playing with Fire

Power Play

# Sweet Valley HIGH®

## Power Play

WRITTEN BY KATE WILLIAM

CREATED BY

FRANCINE PASCAL

Published by Laurel-Leaf
an imprint of Random House Children's Books
a division of Random House, Inc.
New York



Originally produced by Cloverdale Press.
Originally published by Bantam Books, New York, in 1984.

Laurel-Leaf and colophon are registered trademarks of
Random House, Inc.
Sweet Valley High® is a registered trademark of Francine Pascal
Conceived by Francine Pascal

Visit us on the Web! www.randomhouse.com/teens

Educators and librarians, for a variety of teaching tools, visit us at
www.randomhouse.com/teachers

*Library of Congress Cataloging-in-Publication Data*
William, Kate.
Power play / written by Kate William ; created by
Francine Pascal.—1st Laurel-Leaf ed.
p. cm.—(Sweet Valley High ; 4)
Summary: Elizabeth and her twin sister Jessica become locked in a power
play when Elizabeth nominates an unlikely candidate to Sweet Valley
High's snobby sorority.
ISBN 978-0-440-42265-5 (pbk.)
[1. Prejudices—Fiction. 2. Twins—Fiction. 3. Sisters—Fiction. 4. High
schools—Fiction. 5. Schools—Fiction.] I. Pascal, Francine. II. Title.
PZ7.W65549Po 2008
[Fic]—dc22
2007034197

RL: 6
August 2008
Printed in the United States of America
10 9 8 7 6 5 4 3 2 1
First Laurel-Leaf Edition

Random House Children's Books Supports the First Amendment
and celebrates the right to read.

# CHAPTER 1

Elizabeth Wakefield was enjoying her lunch in the Sweet Valley High courtyard on a sunny afternoon–along with her best friend, Enid Rollins; her boyfriend, Todd Wilkins; and their friend Winston Egbert–when her twin sister, Jessica, flitted in out of nowhere and dropped a pink clipboard right on top of her salad.

"Here! Sign this!" Jessica said, perching on an empty chair at the circular table.

She tossed her blond hair in the sun and held out a pen to her sister. Both the Wakefield twins were wearing blue today–Jessica a skinny-strapped sundress, Elizabeth a plain T-shirt–so their blue-green eyes stood out like the

Pacific Ocean against white sand. The only difference was that Jessica's eyes were full of hopeful self-confidence, while Elizabeth's contained pure irritation.

"Hello to you, too, Jess," she said, removing the clipboard from her lunch. A piece of lettuce stuck to the back and she picked it off with her fingers. "What am I signing?"

"I'm starting a new club, and the SVH student handbook says I need at least twelve members," Jessica stated. "I've got ten, so . . ."

"What kind of club?" Enid asked, leaning across the table for a glimpse of the clipboard.

"It's called the Sweet Valley High Beautification Committee. The Beauties, for short," Jessica added with a camera-worthy smile.

Todd snorted a laugh and soda came out of his nose. He quickly covered it up with a napkin, but the damage was done.

"Oh, that's attractive." Jessica grimaced, wrinkling her button nose.

Elizabeth smirked. As if her tall, shaggy-brown-haired, ridiculously handsome boyfriend could ever be anything *but* attractive. Even with soda coming out of his nose.

"Sorry. Just . . . the Beauties?" Todd asked, his brown eyes sparkling.

"Well, if the name fits . . . ," Jessica said.

"I'd say it does," Winston said, practically drooling in Jessica's lap, as always.

Elizabeth looked at Enid and they both rolled their eyes. She scanned the list of ten signatures, including Jessica's own at the top, and saw that Jessica's best friends, Lila Fowler and Cara Walker, had already joined up, as well as seven of the other most gorgeous and popular girls at SVH.

"What, exactly, will the Sweet Valley High Beautification Committee do?" Elizabeth asked, hesitant to sign up for anything that had been schemed up by Jessica.

"We're going to clean this dump up!" Jessica said, wide-eyed.

Elizabeth glanced around at the pristine lawn, the palm trees swaying in the breeze, the gleaming windows, and the bright red SVH Gladiators banner strung across the square.

"Yeah. It's like a total ghetto in here," Elizabeth joked.

"It *so* is," Jessica agreed, missing Elizabeth's sarcastic tone. "Did you see what Palisades looked like when we were there for the tennis match? Freshly planted flower beds, new doormats outside every door in their school colors, lockers all painted blue and yellow for school spirit. They put us to shame. So me and Cara and everyone have decided do some home improvement projects here. You know, restore some pride in our school."

Suddenly, the obvious motivation for this little club hit Elizabeth like a whack to the back of the head. She placed the clipboard aside and turned to fully face her sister, one eyebrow raised.

"Jess . . . this doesn't have anything to do with the upcoming Miss SVH contest, does it?" she asked.

"Oh, right!" Enid said. "I knew there was more."

Jessica shot Enid a look of death. "Lizzie, I have no idea what you're talking about."

"Oh, just that 'annoying' new rule that every contestant for Miss SVH has to have at least eight hours a week of community service," Elizabeth said, knowing beyond a doubt that she was right. "It seems kind of coincidental that your sudden need to beautify SVH coincides with that tiny announcement."

Jessica's expression darkened. "You know, Liz, if you don't want to join my club, you can just say so," she snapped, snatching the clipboard. "You don't have to be so rude about it."

"No! No, Jess. I'll join," Elizabeth said, reaching for the clipboard. "I think it sounds like a good idea. If, you know, you actually do what you say you're going to do."

"Nice to know you think I'm a total flake," Jessica grumbled. But she handed the clipboard over anyway.

Elizabeth quickly signed her name and handed the clipboard to Enid.

"Wait!" Jessica said. "You don't have to–"

"What? I'd like to help beautify our school," Enid said as she signed her name.

Elizabeth knew that her sister wasn't Enid's biggest fan and probably didn't consider her worthy of an exclusive, "beautiful" club. Enid was smart and shy and wore Old Navy to school, while all Jessica's friends were vapid, aloof, and designer-clad. But if Elizabeth was going to be in this club, she was going to have a friendly face there with her.

"Besides, you said you needed twelve," Elizabeth reminded Jessica.

Jessica hesitated as Enid finished. "Fine," she said finally. She took her clipboard and pen back and stood, smoothing her skirt. "I'll let you girls know when the first meeting will be held."

"Wait! I want to join!" Winston said, getting up. He pushed his thick glasses up on his nose and stood awkwardly.

"You?" Jessica said with a laugh. "Thanks anyway, Win, but I've already got my twelve signatures. Besides, I think we're better off keeping this an all-girls thing."

"But that's discrimination!" Winston protested.

Jessica smirked and held out the clipboard. "Fine, if you want all the guys in school calling you a *beauty,* then that's your prerogative."

Winston turned beet red and touched the back of his neck under his mane of curly brown hair. Elizabeth had to hand it to Jessica. She knew exactly which cards to play when it came to Winston.

"On second thought, maybe I'll just go out for wrestling," Winston said, casually flexing his nonexistent muscles.

"Good decision," Jessica said. "Later!"

She twiddled her fingers and sauntered away, with half the male population of the cafeteria drooling after her as she went.

"Your sister is a piece of work," Todd said, shaking his head.

"Yeah, and she's never done a *day* of work in her life," Elizabeth replied. "I can't wait to see how long this thing actually lasts."

• • •

That afternoon, Elizabeth was Swiffering the Spanish-tile floor in her family's airy kitchen when the phone rang. She recognized Jessica's cell number on the caller ID and was ready for a fight the moment she picked up the phone.

"Jess! You were supposed to be home an hour ago to help me clean the house!" she snapped, clutching the cordless receiver.

"God! Nice way to greet your sister!" Jessica whined. "I was just calling to apologize for running late. Practice went over, and then I had to pick up Mom's dry cleaning and now I'm at the library getting–"

"The library? Now I know you're lying," Elizabeth replied, pushing the Swiffer under the cabinets.

"Fine. Whatever. Don't believe me," Jessica replied stonily.

"You know what? I don't even care where you are as long as you're on your way home. This dinner party thing is really important to Mom and we promised we'd have the house ready."

"Hello? I know this! I was there!" Jessica said. "I'll be home as soon as I can. Leave me the dusting!"

And then she hung up.

*The dusting. Of course. The easiest job of them all,* Elizabeth thought, rolling her eyes. *I'm surprised she didn't offer to arrange the flowers.*

Which, of course, had already been arranged by the

professional florist who had delivered several vases full over an hour ago. Elizabeth sighed and walked into the living room to start vacuuming. Just as she plugged the machine in, the doorbell rang. *More deliveries?* Elizabeth wiped her hands on her jeans and answered the door. Robin Wilson stood on the front step, her arms laden with dry cleaning and a stack of library books.

"Hey, Liz!" Robin half grunted. "Is Jessica here?"

"How do you know I'm not Jessica?" Elizabeth joked in a friendly way.

Robin blushed and looked down at Liz's outfit. "No offense, Liz, but I don't think Jessica's ever dressed like that in her life."

Elizabeth checked out her jeans and frumpy work T-shirt and laughed. "Good point. Come on in. She just called and said she'd be home soon. Here. Let me help you with that."

"Thanks."

Robin tipped the stack of books toward Elizabeth and they slid every which way, but Liz managed to catch them all in her arms. She glanced quickly at the titles.

*Secrets of a Beauty Queen*

*Bonnie Brill's Star-Studded Makeovers*

*Wow Them with Words: How to Make Speeches That Stick*

"What's all this?" Elizabeth asked, placing the books

on the table in the foyer as they walked into the living room.

"Oh, I don't know. Jessica asked me to pick them up," Robin said. She slung the dry cleaning over the back of the couch and Elizabeth recognized a few of her mother's power suits.

Elizabeth paused. Robin was picking up their mother's cleaning? And hitting the library for Jessica? Hadn't Jessica just told her those were the errands *she* was running? Robin sat down on the couch, pulled a Snickers bar out of her bag, and tore it open.

"Want some?" she offered.

"No, thanks," Elizabeth said.

"You don't mind, do you? I'm starving," Robin said.

"No. Please. Go ahead," Elizabeth said. She watched as Robin practically inhaled the candy bar.

"I probably shouldn't even be eating this," Robin said sheepishly, apparently noticing Elizabeth's stare. "But when I get a craving for chocolate, I can't help myself."

"Join the club," Elizabeth joked, not wanting Robin to think she was judging her.

Which she wasn't–she didn't think. She just wondered if Robin might be a bit healthier and happier if she carried an apple around with her instead of a candy bar for times like these. At least she wouldn't feel like she had to make excuses for her snacking. Robin was a pretty girl, with her thick brown hair and sparkling brown eyes, but she was a bit overweight–and self-conscious about it. Sometimes Elizabeth couldn't help thinking that Robin could be a serious hottie if she'd just stop giving in to her cravings so easily.

Though Elizabeth and Jessica had been born with skinny genes, they had also been brought up on a healthy diet and knew how to eat right and when to indulge. Thus their perfect size-four figures and healthy, glowing skin. Elizabeth was four minutes older, but she and Jessica were identical down to the tiny dimple each had in her left cheek. Although they wore the same size, they never dressed alike, except for the matching lavalieres they wore on gold chains around their necks–presents from their parents on their sixteenth birthday.

The only way a stranger could tell them apart was by a tiny beauty mark on Elizabeth's right shoulder. Their close friends also knew that Elizabeth always wore a watch, while Jessica never did. Jess felt that things didn't really start until she got there, anyway. And if she happened to be late, let them wait.

That "let them wait" attitude was coming into play right now, and with each passing moment, Elizabeth was growing more and more tense.

"Look, Robin, Jessica may have gotten held up somewhere," she said, glancing at her watch. "Maybe you should try calling her later, or–"

"That's okay, Liz," Robin said, hoisting herself off the couch. "I just wanted to drop this stuff off for her, anyway."

"Robin, why exactly are you running Jessica's errands for her?" Elizabeth asked.

"Oh, well, she said she had something important to do and I was free, so . . ." Robin shrugged and smiled. "What are best friends for?"

Elizabeth felt a sting in her heart. She knew that Jessica considered Robin her best friend in the same way she considered Winston Egbert the love of her life. Her sister was just using Robin, and Robin was falling for it like a log.

"Anyway, I'll get out of your way," Robin said, turning for the door. "Oh, wait! Actually, can I ask you something?"

"Sure," Elizabeth replied.

"Have you heard about this new club Jessica's starting up? The Sweet Valley High Beautification Committee?" Robin asked hopefully.

Elizabeth's cheeks flushed. She had a feeling she knew where this was going. "Sure. Yeah. She made me sign up for it," she said lightly.

"Well, is membership still open, do you know?

Because I'd like to join," Robin said. "It sounds like it could be really cool."

Yep. Exactly where she'd thought it was going. Ever since Robin had moved to Sweet Valley, her main goals had been befriending Jessica and fitting in with the popular crowd. The only problem was that she was a nice girl. And nice girls were just not cutthroat or manipulative enough to succeed at such plans.

"Oh, well . . ."

Elizabeth had no idea what to say. She knew that if Jessica had hesitated in allowing Enid into her club, she'd definitely balk at having Robin. And this *was* Jessica's thing. Who was Elizabeth to invite people to join the Beauties? But then again, just because that was Jessica's attitude, that didn't make it right. Anyone who wanted to join the committee and help beautify the school should be able to.

"As far as I know, yes, membership is still open," Elizabeth replied finally.

"Really? Do you think I could join? I mean, I was surprised when Jessica didn't mention it to me herself, but then, she's probably been so busy setting the whole thing up . . ."

"As soon as I know when the first meeting's going to be, I'll let you know," Elizabeth told her, resolved, as always, to do the right thing no matter how big a fit her sister might throw.

"Thanks so much, Liz!" Robin said, beaming now. "I can't wait. Tell Jessica I'll call her later!"

"Okay."

Elizabeth was just opening the door for Robin when Jessica burst through, already making excuses.

"I know! I know! I'm *sorry*!" she rambled as she barreled right past both Liz and Robin. "All I have to do is run upstairs and check one little thing on my e-mail and then–"

"Hey, Jess!" Robin said brightly.

Jessica did a double take. She dropped a huge shopping bag onto the floor by the stairs and shrank backward as Robin hurtled toward her for a hug. Jessica patted the girl on the back as Robin nearly squeezed the life out of her.

"Oh. Hi, Robin," she grunted.

"Omigod, Jess! I'm so excited about the beautification committee!" Robin trilled, taking a step back. "When's the first meeting going to be?"

Jessica blanched. She glanced helplessly at Elizabeth, then back at Robin's glowing face. "Oh, um, I don't know yet."

"That's okay," Robin said. "Just call me when you do! I already have so many ideas for projects!"

"That's great, Robin," Elizabeth said when Jessica seemed too stunned to reply.

"Yeah. Great," Jess said flatly.

"I'll see you guys later!" Robin said. Then she bounded out the front door, slamming it behind her.

Jessica straightened up and pushed her sunglasses back into her hair. "*What* was *that*?"

"*That* was your best friend," Elizabeth said as she turned and walked back into the living room.

"My best friend? Please," Jessica said.

"Well, she thinks she is," Elizabeth said, snagging her mother's clean clothes to hang up in the front closet. "Where have you been, Jessica? Because I know you weren't out picking up dry cleaning and books," she said, gesturing at the stack on the table.

"I had stuff to do, okay?" Jessica said, grabbing her shopping bag.

"At the mall, of course," Elizabeth said. "Is that where you got the necklace?"

Jessica's fingers flew to an intricate, colorfully beaded necklace just shorter than her lavaliere chain. "This?"

"Yeah, that," Elizabeth said. "It looks expensive. How did you pay for that?"

"What are you, the CIA?" Jessica snapped.

"Just curious," Elizabeth said, raising her hands. *Since I happen to know you spent all your allowance on clothes last weekend,* she thought.

"Well, Agent Wakefield, FYI, Lila gave this to me," Jessica said. "Her aunt sent it to her from New York. It's one of a kind."

Elizabeth eyed her sister dubiously. "If it's one of a kind, why would Lila give it to you?"

"She's not into beads," Jessica said. "She's a Fowler. It's platinum and diamonds or nothing."

"Oh. Of course," Elizabeth said wryly. "Well, I'm very happy for you and your one-of-a-kind necklace, but I don't appreciate having to clean the whole house by myself. Not to mention having to make excuses to your so-called best friend."

"For that, I am *truly* sorry," Jessica said, rolling her eyes. "No one wants to have to spend too much time alone with the Wilsonator."

"The Wilsonator?" Elizabeth asked.

"Just a nickname," Jessica said, glancing at her reflection in the foyer mirror. "We'd never say it to her face, of course."

"Of course not," Elizabeth replied.

"What was she talking about the Beauties for, anyway?" Jessica asked.

*Here we go,* Elizabeth thought, holding her breath. "She wants to join."

Jessica laughed cruelly. "Yeah, right."

"Why not? It's a service club, right? Shouldn't anyone who wants to do service be able to join?" Elizabeth asked, walking back into the living room and grabbing the vacuum cleaner.

"Liz, it's an *exclusive* service club. Exclusively mine. As in, I get to decide who joins," Jessica said, following her.

"Too bad, since I already promised to bring her to the first meeting," Elizabeth said. Then she flicked the vacuum on to drown out her sister's indignant cries.

"Liz! Elizabeth!" Jessica shouted. She walked over to the wall and yanked out the plug. The vacuum instantly died. "You did not promise her that!"

"Yes, I did," Elizabeth replied calmly.

"Are you insane?" Jessica cried, throwing her hands up.

Elizabeth was all innocence as she gazed back at her sister. She hadn't lived with Jessica Wakefield for sixteen years without picking up a few dramatic skills.

"What? What's the problem?" she asked.

"That cow? A Beauty?" Jessica blurted out.

"You know, inappropriate nickname aside, are you really going to tell me that one of the requirements to be in a flower-planting club is physical beauty?" Elizabeth asked facetiously.

"It is for this one! All my friends are in it! They're not going to want to be associated with the Wilsonator,"

Jessica protested. "This is supposed to be, like, an up-scale beautification committee. Like those women from the country club who plant the gardens downtown every spring. I wanted to project an image!"

"Image? That doesn't seem to bother you when she carries your books and cleaning around for you," Elizabeth replied.

Jessica sighed. "Look, Liz, Robin's okay, but she's just not Beauty material. Besides, she's already taking, like, a zillion honors courses and she works with her mom and volunteers on weekends. She won't have enough time to devote to the committee. I'm only thinking of the club."

"Uh-huh," Elizabeth said sarcastically. "Well, I'm in all the same honors classes as Robin and I have The Oracle, but you had no problem letting me join."

"God. Any chance to remind me how smart you are, huh?" Jessica sneered.

"Yeah. That was obviously my point," Elizabeth said, rolling her eyes. "All I'm saying is, I think the club could benefit from someone like Robin. She just said she already has tons of ideas, and I, for one, can't wait to hear them."

Jessica's face turned pink with rage. Elizabeth knew that the fit was coming and braced herself for it. "I cannot believe you, Elizabeth Wakefield. You can't just swoop in and hijack my new club! I put a lot of thought into the membership and I'm not going to let just anyone infiltrate it!"

"You make it sound like an army maneuver, Jess. What's the big deal?" Elizabeth asked.

"The big deal? The big deal is you're cracked if you think someone like Lila Fowler is going to hang out with someone like Robin Wilson!" Jessica screeched. "And forget the nickname 'the Beauties'! They'll be calling us the Butterballs by the end of the week!"

Elizabeth rolled her eyes again. Sometimes it really irked her how the only thing Jessica cared about was what other people thought. Didn't she ever have a single inkling about other people's *feelings*?

"You know what? This is a pointless argument," she said. "I promised Robin, and that's that. She's going to be a Beauty."

"Yeah. That's what you think," Jessica said, whirling around and storming out of the room.

Elizabeth's heart skipped a beat. She didn't like that tone.

"What's that supposed to mean?" she asked, following her sister.

Jessica stopped halfway up the stairs and turned to

glare at Elizabeth. "You're the smart one. You figure it out!"

Then she stomped up the rest of the stairs and slammed the door to her room so hard the walls trembled. Elizabeth sighed and shook her head. She guessed this meant she really was going to do all the cleaning by herself.

# CHAPTER 2

"ALL RIGHT, LET'S get the first meeting of the Sweet Valley High Beautification Committee started!" Jessica said as she handed out the last of her carefully crafted SVHBC handbooks. As she faced the room, she was happy to note that her do-gooding sister and her project of the moment, Robin, had not, in fact, shown up. Maybe in the midst of all her martyrish thoughts, Elizabeth had forgotten about the actual meeting. The school handbook stated that Jessica had to have twelve members join, not that all twelve had to show up for every meeting. Perfection.

Still, it might be a good idea to keep this first meeting short but sweet, just in case. She had her anti-Robin plan in place, but she would prefer to avoid a nasty scene at her inaugural meeting, if possible.

"Okay, as you all know, I'm Jessica Wakefield, and as founder of this club, I will also be serving as president," Jessica announced.

Cara Walker flicked her straight black hair over her shoulder and raised her hand.

"Yes, Cara?" Jessica asked.

"Will there be elections for a vice president and secretary and all that?" Cara asked.

"Sure," Jessica said. "But not today. Today, all I wanted to do was pass out the handbooks and let you know that our first project will be–"

At that moment, the classroom door opened and in barreled Elizabeth, out of breath, with Robin Wilson right on her heels. Robin was positively heaving for air, her skin splotched with red from exertion. The inside of Jessica's mouth suddenly tasted sour. So, a nasty scene it would be.

"Sorry we're late," Elizabeth said, starting into the room. "What did we miss?"

Jessica stepped in front of her sister and her tubby cohort, effectively blocking them from the desks. Behind her, she could already hear her friends murmuring about Robin. Murmuring and snickering.

"You missed this," Jessica said, holding out a handbook to Elizabeth.

"'The Sweet Valley High Beautification Committee Handbook,'" Elizabeth read. She raised her eyebrows, impressed. "Wow. You've really put a lot of work into this, Jess."

So innocent. So naïve.

"Thanks. Check out page one. The bylaws," Jessica said.

"Hi, Jess!" Robin mouthed over Elizabeth's shoulder, having finally caught her breath.

Jessica simply looked away.

"'Founding members,'" Elizabeth read quietly, glancing down the list of twelve names. Then her jaw slackened as she read on. When she looked up at Jessica again, her blue eyes had turned to steel. "Any student wishing to join after the initial founding members must be approved by a two-thirds majority of the founding members? You can't do that!"

"Sure I can," Jessica said, sauntering over to her messenger bag. She pulled out the SVH student handbook and offered it to Liz. "Read the section on the formation of new clubs. It says I have the right to make up a handbook and the handbook can contain any governing rules for the club that I like. Including membership restrictions."

Normally, Jessica detested how out-of-date and backward the administration of SVH could sometimes be. But their neglecting to update the extracurricular section of the student handbook for at least twenty years had definitely helped her out in this case. The rule was archaic and maybe even supported discrimination, as Winston would have put it, but it was there in black and white.

"I cannot believe you're doing this," Elizabeth said under her breath.

"Doing what? I just want to make sure that everyone in the Beauties really wants to be here," Jessica said. "If you want to join, Robin, you'll have to fill out an application." She glanced over her shoulder. "Lila?"

Lila Fowler rose from her desk in the front row in one graceful motion, pulling out a packet of at least ten pages stapled together. She handed this to Robin with a barely disguised sneer before returning to her seat and tucking her miniskirt beneath her slim, tan legs.

"Take that home and fill it out," Jessica told Robin. "I'll stop by your house later tonight to pick it up. Say, sevenish? You should have it all done by then, right?"

Robin flipped furiously through the pages, blanching as she took in the essay questions.

"I . . ."

"Problem?" Lila asked, checking the ends of her

perfect light brown hair for splits. "Because if it's too much–"

"Oh, no!" Robin blurted out with a smile. "Not at all. I'll go home right now and start on it. Thanks, Jess!"

Elizabeth gaped, as if she couldn't believe that Robin was thanking Jessica for giving her what amounted to hours of extra homework. But Jessica wasn't surprised. She knew how much Robin wanted her approval and friendship. She also knew, however, that Robin would never survive what she had planned for her. Not by a long shot.

"Bye, Robin!" Jessica trilled.

Robin smacked sideways into the doorjamb before bouncing out into the hallway and closing the door. The moment she was gone, the room erupted with laughter. Only Elizabeth and Enid didn't seem to appreciate the joke.

"Now. Where were we?" Jessica asked. "Oh, right. Our first project."

She glanced at her sister, who was still standing near the door, silently fuming. If Jessica knew anything about Elizabeth, she knew the war Elizabeth was having with her conscience right now. Elizabeth wanted more than anything to storm out–to make a point. And while Jessica would have liked to have her sister in her new club, part of her wished Liz would just go. It would make what she was going to do with Robin much easier.

"Are you going to sit, or what?" Jessica said in a challenging way.

Elizabeth stared at Jessica, her eyes narrowed, and Jessica realized that Elizabeth had just come to the same conclusion she had. She could either go and leave Robin to the wolves or stay and try to protect her. Liz took a deep breath, turned toward the desks, and sat next to Enid.

Jessica smirked. Her sister had just declared war.

• • •

Right around seven, Jessica stood at the front door of Robin's house, with Cara and Lila at her sides. It was quite a nice house. One of the newer, bigger ones in town, with a meticulously kept front yard, Spanish-style doorways, and a red-tile roof. It might have earned Robin a few points, if Jessica were at all inclined to give her any.

Jessica rang the bell again and waited. Lila sighed impatiently. The girl did not like to waste her time.

"Maybe she's not home," Cara suggested.

"Please. Like she has anywhere else to be," Jessica joked.

Just then, the door swung open. "Hi, Jess!" Robin beamed at her with excitement. Then she noticed the other girls and her smile faltered. "Lila, Cara. What are you guys doing here?"

"Making sure you don't eat our friend?" Lila said under her breath. Cara laughed and Jessica stepped inside the wide foyer. Luckily, Robin didn't seem to have heard Lila's comment. No, Robin did not belong in the Beauties, but if Jessica could avoid being snide to the poor girl's face, she would. Unless, of course, Robin became a real problem.

"Lila and Cara have been elected vice president and secretary of the Beauties," Jessica informed Robin. After the nasty scene had ended so quickly, she had decided to hold elections after all. "They wanted to come along, since this is official business."

"Did you finish the application?" Cara asked with obvious interest.

"Yep! Got it right here," Robin said, handing over the ten pages.

Jessica swallowed hard as she flipped through them. All Robin's answers had been neatly printed out on the pages provided. So much for the application slowing her down.

"Can I get you guys something to eat or drink? My mom's been experimenting with cheesecakes lately, so we have, like, a ton in all different flavors," Robin offered.

Robin's mother was a professional chef and ran a new and already successful catering company in town. *Neither of which can be helping with Robin's weight issues,* Jessica thought.

"Do you know how many calories there are in one slice of cheesecake?" Lila sniffed. "Please."

Robin's face fell and she looked down at her shoes.

"Thanks for the offer, but we all just ate," Jessica told her. She handed Robin's application to Cara, who immediately started reading. "As long as that's in order, you will officially be considered for membership in the Beauties," Jessica said, back to business.

The smile of pure happiness on Robin's face was so heartbreakingly sincere and grateful it almost made Jessica change her mind about her whole plan. Almost, but not quite.

"Omigosh! Yay!" Robin exclaimed, hugging Jessica. "Thank you! Thank you! Thank you!"

"No one said you were a member yet," Lila reminded her.

Robin cleared her throat and stepped back, serious again. "Right. Of course. Is there something else I need to do?"

Jessica smiled at Lila and Cara, who both smiled back.

"Well, like I said at the meeting, we want to make sure that all the members of the Beauties *truly* want to be there," Jessica said. "This club is going to do a lot of hard work, and we want to know that our members are up to it."

"Oh, I am. I've always been a hard worker," Robin said brightly.

"Like a mule," Lila said under her breath.

Robin heard that one and her face fell, but she refocused on Jessica and smiled.

"Well, we're going to find out," Jessica continued as if Lila hadn't spoken. "We've developed a series of tasks for you, and if you complete the tasks, you will be welcomed as a member of the Beauties."

"Tasks?" Robin appeared uncertain.

"Some of them might be kind of hard," Cara said.

"Exactly, so if you want to back out now, we'll totally understand," Jessica added.

"Oh, no. Nothing would be too hard, you guys. Nothing. I'll do whatever you want me to do," Robin vowed.

"Good. That's what we like to hear," Jessica said, even though she would have much preferred if Robin had just given up right then. "Meet us in the locker room tomorrow at the beginning of our lunch period. Don't be late."

"Got it," Robin said with a nod. "I'll be there."

She walked Jessica, Lila, and Cara to the door and waved enthusiastically at them as they made their way down the walk.

"Unbelievable," Lila said, shaking her head in wonder as she climbed behind the wheel of her gold Mercedes convertible. "Does that girl have no shame?"

"Well, we're going to find out," Jessica said, slipping her sunglasses on. "Tomorrow."

• • •

"Jess! Jessica! Hello!" Elizabeth shouted.

Jessica was on the elliptical trainer in their father's study, her iPod cranked up so loud she was definitely doing permanent damage to her ears. Elizabeth had to step right in front of her and wave her hand to get her attention.

"What is it?" Jessica said, rolling her eyes as she yanked the earbuds out. "I just reached peak cardio level."

"I just wanted to see what happened at Robin's," Elizabeth said, crossing her arms over her chest. "What did you guys do?"

"Nothing. We picked up her application," Jessica said. "God, Liz. When did you get so paranoid?"

"When you decided to turn your community-beautification club into a sorority," Elizabeth replied.

Jessica rolled her eyes again. "Whatever. Just because I have standards and you don't–"

"I have standards," Elizabeth told her, walking over to their father's desk to toy with the paperweight she'd made him in fourth grade. "Robin just meets all of them."

Jessica snorted a laugh. "Like what?"

"Like she's nice, intelligent, funny, and always there for you," Elizabeth replied, the color rising in her face.

"Geez, Liz. Why don't you just marry the girl, then?" Jessica asked, placing her earbuds back into her ears. "Now, if you don't mind, I'm trying to work on my thighs here."

An earbud fell right out and Jessica cursed under her breath. As Jess started to replace it, Elizabeth saw what the problem was. A pair of fairly large diamond earrings were getting in the way.

"Jess!"

"What!" Jessica said, hand over her heart.

"Where did you get those earrings?" Elizabeth asked, taking a closer look.

Jessica blew out a deep breath. "You scared me half to

death. You shouldn't do that to a person when they're working out!"

"Jessica–"

"Elizabeth," Jessica said, mimicking Liz's no-nonsense tone. "I got them from Lila, Miss Jewelry Police. Her aunt sent them to her and she already has a pair just like them, so she gave them to me. Aren't they spectacular?"

"That's an understatement," Elizabeth said. She placed her paperweight down and narrowed her eyes. "Jess, don't you think it's a little weird that Lila has suddenly become so generous?"

"What's weird about it? She *is* my best friend," Jessica replied. "If I had something I didn't want, I'd give it to her. Not that she'd ever need anything of mine."

"Of course not," Elizabeth said wryly.

Jessica was, of course, known more for taking things–especially from Elizabeth–than she was for giving stuff away.

"So, you never told me. How was Robin's *application*?" Elizabeth asked, her emphasis clearly indicating how much she disapproved of her twin's behavior.

"It was fine," Jessica said blithely. "But that was just phase one. Tomorrow, we start phase two."

"Phase two? Why don't I like the sound of that?" Elizabeth asked.

"Your paranoia again?" Jessica suggested. "Do you mind, Liz? I really want to finish this workout."

"So you're not going to tell me what you're doing to-morrow," Elizabeth said suspiciously.

"Nope. You'll just have to wait and find out with the rest of the school," Jessica replied. She finally succeeded in getting the earbuds past her big sparkling earrings and cranked the volume up even more. Elizabeth shook her head, knowing when Jessica deemed a conversation over, and walked out.

"The rest of the school," Elizabeth said to herself once she was alone in the hallway. "I *really* don't like the sound of that."

# CHAPTER 3

ELIZABETH SLAMMED HER locker as yet another crowd of juniors trailed by her, heading down the steps and out the front door of the school. At least three of them, she knew, had lunch this period–same as she did. So what were they all doing walking away from the cafeteria? Seniors were allowed off campus at lunch, but juniors were not.

"Todd!" Elizabeth called out, spotting him over the crowd. "What's going on?"

"You haven't heard?" he asked, his brown eyes concerned.

Elizabeth's heart thumped extra-hard. Why did

Jessica's face suddenly float across her mind with that twist of foreboding? "Heard what?"

"Robin Wilson's working out on the track, and apparently Jessica has made sure that every junior and senior will be there to catch the show," he said.

"What? Please tell me you're kidding," Elizabeth said. She felt as if her life were flashing before her eyes. How could Jessica do this?

But the joyful snickers of another pack of kids jogging by them confirmed his story.

"We have to get out there," Elizabeth said, turning toward the door.

"Wait! But then won't we just be part of the, you know, the problem or whatever?" Todd said.

"Not if we get her the heck out of there," Elizabeth replied. "Come on!"

Together, Elizabeth and Todd sprinted out the front door of the school, skirting the clumps of slower kids. From across the parking lot and the street, Elizabeth could already see that the bleachers around the football stadium were filling up. The sight only made her run harder. She crossed the street against the light and burst through the gate that led to the track, which circumscribed the football field. Sure enough, there was Robin on the other side of the track, jogging away under the hot afternoon sun.

"Go, Robin!" someone in the stands shouted.

"Don't fall down, Wilson! You'll dent the track!"

Elizabeth whirled around at this evil remark, more than ready to tear out the heart of whomever had made it, and spotted Bruce Patman lounging back against the fence.

"Real mature, Bruce," she snapped. "Daddy would be so proud."

The sneer fell off Bruce's face. If there was one thing that got to him, it was somebody's invoking the name of his staid and well-respected father.

"I am going to *kill* my sister," Elizabeth fumed to Todd. She spotted Jessica easily. Jess was standing on the bottom bleacher with Lila and Cara, holding a stop-watch. Elizabeth stormed over to the beyond-cruel threesome. "This is disgusting, Jessica, even for you," she snapped.

"I know. I can't believe she would be caught dead in shorts with all those nasty pockmarks on her legs," Lila sneered.

"Not her! You!" Elizabeth shouted, earning a few "ooohs" from the crowd. "What is the matter with you guys? How can you do this to her? To anyone?"

"Come on, Liz. Robin could benefit from a little exercise," Jessica replied snidely. "Maybe if she does another hundred and thirty laps she'll actually drop a pound or two."

There was laughter from the peanut gallery behind

them. Elizabeth couldn't believe that her peers could be so mean. She turned to glare at the crowd and was mollified, at least, to see that a lot of the kids just looked confused about why they were there, and some were already leaving. Only Jessica's band of followers seemed to be really into the sideshow.

"Honestly, Jess? Right now, I'm ashamed to be related to you," Elizabeth said under her breath. Then she tromped down the bleacher steps as Robin rounded the final turn and headed toward her. "Robin! That's it! You've done enough."

Robin's face was so red, her breathing so short and labored, Elizabeth was sure she was going to faint. Robin immediately slowed to a walk and started to cough.

"Are you all right? You don't look so good," Elizabeth said, offering her arm.

"I've . . . never looked . . . great . . . in shorts," Robin joked between gasps.

Elizabeth smiled. Unreal. She was impressed that Robin could joke at a moment like this. She wrapped her arm around Robin's waist to help her walk it off. The crowd in the bleachers, mercifully, started to disperse. Elizabeth saw Jessica shoot her an irritated look before flouncing off with her friends.

"Why did you do it, Robin? Haven't you ever heard of 'just say no?' " Liz asked.

Robin's face showed pure astonishment. "Jessica said I had to prove I really wanted to be a Beauty," she said. "It's all about dedication and hard work."

"Yeah, maybe. But it's not about jogging," Elizabeth replied.

Robin laughed, clutching her side. "Yeah, well, I did tell her and Lila and Cara that I'd do whatever they asked me to do. I can't back down now. I'll look like a total loser."

Elizabeth swallowed hard. Whatever they asked her to do? That couldn't be good. What else did Jessica have in mind?

"Anyway, I only have to do this for the rest of the week. So that's just two more lunch periods," Robin said, walking a bit straighter now.

"Wait. You have to do this for the rest of the week?" Elizabeth asked, following her. "Robin, come on. This is insane. Is it really that important to you to be a Beauty?"

Elizabeth knew that Robin wanted to be popular, but getting into Jessica's stupid club couldn't be the only way.

But when Robin paused and turned to look at

Elizabeth, her expression was quite serious. "Liz, you don't understand. Being in this club is more important than anything."

Apparently, Robin was convinced that the Beauties *were* the only way.

• • •

Elizabeth waited in the locker room for Robin at the end of lunch on Friday, with a cold bottle of water all ready for her friend. As soon as the door opened, she was on her feet.

"I can't believe you did it, Robin. I'm so impressed," Elizabeth said, holding out the water.

Robin took it and dropped heavily down onto the bench, looking defeated. Elizabeth was surprised. This wasn't what she'd been expecting. She had thought that Robin would be jovial and triumphant after surviving Jessica's challenge.

"Thanks," Robin mumbled, then sipped the water.

"What's the matter? You should be bouncing off the walls after making it through the last few days," Elizabeth said, sitting next to her. "After that, you can handle anything."

Robin gave her a rueful smile. "Anything except tomorrow."

"Tomorrow? What's tomorrow?" Elizabeth asked, not entirely sure she wanted the answer.

"The beach," Robin said. She placed the bottle down and covered her face with her hands. "Oh God. There's no way I can do this."

"Do what?" Elizabeth asked. Her heart was starting to pound with trepidation. What was Jessica going to make the girl do now, tread water for an hour?

"You know this volleyball fund-raiser Jessica's doing for the Beauties?" Robin asked, lowering her hands but slumping miserably.

Elizabeth blinked. She had thought she'd overheard Jessica saying something about a volleyball game this weekend at the beach, but she'd said nothing to Liz about a fund-raiser. Nice to be included as a member of the club.

"Yeah," Elizabeth lied.

"Well, I have to participate! Which wouldn't even be that bad except . . . except . . ."

"Except what?" Elizabeth prompted.

"She says all the players have to wear two-pieces!" Robin wailed, covering her face again. "I can't show up in front of half the athletes at SVH in a bikini! I'll die!"

Elizabeth was appalled. Just when she thought Jessica could do no worse, Jessica came up with something even more horrific than before.

"What do you mean, 'half the athletes'?" Elizabeth asked.

"That's who we're playing," Robin sniffled. "Football players, tennis players, basketball players. Only all the hottest guys in school."

Elizabeth stood up, no longer able to sit still. "I can't believe her," she said, pacing in front of Robin. "I mean, a charity volleyball game is one thing, but to mandate that everyone has to wear a two-piece, that's just sexist and–"

She stopped rambling. Something she had just said had caused an epiphany.

"Robin, wait a sec. Did Jessica say a bikini or a two-piece?" she asked, then held her breath.

Robin thought about it for a moment, her eyes trained up at the ceiling. "Two-piece. She definitely said two-piece."

Elizabeth grinned. "Perfect. Meet me out in the parking lot right after school."

"Why?" Robin asked, wide-eyed.

Elizabeth grabbed her book bag as the bell rang, ending the period. "Because you and I are going shopping."

• • •

Saturday morning, Elizabeth stuck by Robin as dozens of kids from Sweet Valley set up camp at the beach and took their spots around the sand volleyball court to watch. As Jessica, Lila, and Cara stood at a safe distance to observe with glee, Robin stepped out of her shorts and pulled off her T-shirt, revealing the modest two-piece tankini she had purchased the day before. It was totally slimming and flattering, if Elizabeth did say so herself. Robin didn't even seem all that self-conscious in it, which made Elizabeth smile. Of course, nothing was better than the look of shock and anger that overcame Jessica at the sight of Robin's suit. The moment she saw Robin and Elizabeth, she stormed right over to them.

"Robin, that is not a bikini," Jessica said, clearly trying not to sound as annoyed as she felt.

"You didn't say 'bikini,' Jess. You said 'two-piece,'" Elizabeth replied, taking off her T-shirt dress to reveal her own tankini. "Now, when do we start the fund-raiser game? That is what today is all about, isn't it?"

Jessica looked like she was about to blow up–a look Elizabeth knew all too well–but somehow, she contained herself. She even forced a smile. "Yes, it is," she said. "So why don't we all take the court?"

Elizabeth and Robin followed Jessica to the sand court and took their places alongside Jessica, Cara, Lila, and Enid. On the other side of the court was a team made up of some of Sweet Valley High's best athletes–

Todd Wilkins, Ken Matthews, and Bruce Patman among them.

"This is going to be a slaughter," Enid said under her breath. "Did Jessica want to get us humiliated?"

"No. I think she only wanted to humiliate one person, but so far that hasn't worked out," Elizabeth whispered.

Todd served the ball and the game was on. Within five minutes, it was clear that this was not going to be pretty. Not only were Lila, Enid, and Robin all fairly inept, but Bruce seemed to delight in shooting one ball after another right at Robin, none of which she returned. They either hit the ground at her feet, spraying sand into her face, or bounced off her hands and flew into the crowd.

"Way to go, Wilson," Bruce jeered. "You'd think with a body that size you'd be able to cover more of the court, not less."

Robin blushed but ignored him and somehow managed to get through the game. The Beauties lost fifteen to two, but the crowd seemed to appreciate the effort nonetheless.

At the end of the day, Robin seemed relaxed. Happy even. Everyone had picnicked together, chowing down on hot dogs and hamburgers, and then Robin had joined Liz, Todd, Enid, and Enid's boyfriend, George, on their blanket to hang out and swim for a few hours.

"Today was fun," Robin declared as they packed up their stuff.

"Yeah, it actually was," Liz replied. "I knew you could do it, Robin."

"I guess I could," Robin said happily.

"So, I'll drop you off first and then take Enid home," Elizabeth suggested as she pulled her dress over her suit.

"Oh, I don't need a ride home, thanks," Robin said. "Jessica and Lila offered to take me."

"They did?" Elizabeth asked, casting a glance in her sister's direction. Jessica was, of course, flirting with the lifeguard who had just gotten off duty. "You sure? I can take you, no problem."

"I know, but I feel like I've barely had a chance to talk to Jessica all day," Robin said, shouldering her beach bag. It was amazing how Robin was incapable of seeing the bad in Jessica. It was like she wanted to see her as an angel no matter what. "Thanks again for everything, Liz. I'll talk to you later."

"No problem, Robin," Elizabeth replied.

Feeling as if she were watching a lamb on its way to

the slaughter, she watched as her friend made her way up the beach.

• • •

"I'm really impressed with you, Robin," Jessica said as Lila pulled her Mercedes to a stop in front of Robin's house. "We all are."

Robin couldn't even find her voice. Praise from Jessica? Unbelievable. Did this mean the tests were over? Was she finally going to get to be a Beauty?

"You've done everything we asked you to do, and you've done . . . pretty well," Jessica said.

"Thanks," Robin managed to say. She turned toward Jessica on the backseat, forgetting that Lila and Cara were even in the car. "I'm so excited to be a Beauty, you have no idea."

"Eh-eh!" Jessica said, holding up a hand. "We're not quite there yet. There's still one more thing we want you to do."

Robin's heart fell, but she somehow managed to keep the smile on her face. "Oh. Okay. What is it?"

"Cara?" Jessica said.

Cara reached down to the floor and lifted a shoe box, which she passed back to Jessica.

"In this box are the names of fifty of the most gorgeous bachelors at SVH," Jessica said, shaking the box up so that Robin could hear the folded papers rustling inside. "You are to pick one and ask that guy to the seventies dance next Saturday night."

Robin felt as if she were going to throw up. She had never asked out a guy in her life.

"I'm . . . I'm sorry, but . . . what does that have to do with the SVH Beautification Committee?" Robin squeaked. The moment she asked the question, she knew she had made a mistake. Jessica's expression was disapproving, to say the least.

"Robin, in case you haven't noticed, the Beauties are made up of some of the most popular, beautiful girls at SVH," Jessica said. "I know it's not PC or whatever, but we have an image to project. And part of that image is self-confidence. Any self-confident girl can ask out any guy at any time. But if you don't think you can do it . . ."

"No! I can do it!" Robin said automatically. "I'll do it."

Was it just her, or did Jessica look disappointed at that moment? But then she smiled, and the moment passed. "All right, then. Choose," she said, lifting the top of the box with a flourish.

Robin closed her eyes and said a quick prayer that she would pick Winston Egbert or someone equally nice. She put her hand in the box and rooted around for a minute before grasping a piece of paper. Slowly, she unfolded the scrap and the entire world seemed to crumble around her.

"Who did you get?" Lila asked with a laugh in her voice.

Robin swallowed hard against the sudden dryness in her throat. "Bruce Patman."

# CHAPTER 4

ELIZABETH WALKED OUT one of the side doors of Sweet Valley High on Monday afternoon, thinking she might use her rare free moment to check out football practice. She never would have admitted it to anyone, but she loved watching Todd play. There was something so sexy about him in action, colliding with the other players, making those insane acrobatic catches. The tight football pants didn't hurt either.

Blushing, Elizabeth strode around the side of the gym and stopped in her tracks. Robin was sitting on one of the wooden benches in the middle of the grassy area next to the school, staring forlornly into space, her knees pulled up under her chin.

Elizabeth's heart instantly went out to the girl. She looked so lonely and sad. But why? After the way she'd stood up to Jessica's challenges last week and over the weekend, shouldn't she be feeling better about herself by now? She was practically invincible. In fact, in Elizabeth's opinion, she'd put a positive spin on that awful nickname Jessica and the others had given her. The Wilsonator–Girl Indestructible.

"Hey, Robin!" Elizabeth said brightly as she approached, hoping to snap her out of her funk.

Robin looked up and quickly wiped a tear from under her eye. Her chin quivered and she took a deep breath to stop it.

"Robin! What's wrong?" Elizabeth asked, sitting next to her.

Another tear spilled from Robin's eye and she snatched that one away too. "I'm done, Liz," Robin sniffled. "Stick a fork in me."

"What do you mean?" Elizabeth asked.

"I'm never going to be able to do it," Robin muttered, dropping her feet to the ground as she turned in her seat. "I should just quit trying to get into the Beauties now."

Elizabeth's face turned to stone. Jessica. She should have known. Only her dear twin sister could make

Robin this miserable. What had she asked the poor girl to do now?

"You can't quit," Elizabeth said in her best pep-talk voice. "Look how far you've already come! Everyone's beyond impressed."

"Really?" Robin said hopefully.

"Totally," Elizabeth replied. *At least Enid and I are.*

"I just don't understand why they're making me do all this stuff," Robin muttered, looking truly angry for the first time. "If Jessica had just asked me to sign up in the first place, then *I* would have been a founding member too. None of you guys had to do any of this."

"I know," Elizabeth said quietly.

*My sister totally sucks,* she added to herself.

"Why didn't she ask me?" Robin demanded, turning her knees toward Liz's. "I thought we were best friends. But apparently there are at least eleven people she likes better. Including Enid! Who, no offense, I thought Jessica couldn't stand."

*She can't,* Elizabeth thought.

"Listen, Robin, this is just the way Jessica is," Elizabeth said with a shrug. "It's nothing against you." Lie. "She just likes to . . . challenge people. It's her thing." Half truth.

"Well, she's definitely good at it," Robin said ruefully, looking down at her sandals again. "She's come up with the perfect way to challenge me."

Elizabeth swallowed hard and pressed her sweaty palms into the gnarled grain of the wood on either side of her legs. She braced herself for the worst.

"What is it?" she asked. "What did she ask you to do?" She held her breath.

Robin rolled her eyes and then covered her face with her hands, as if she could hardly stand to recall what had happened. "She had me pick a boy's name out of a box, and now I have to ask him to the seventies dance."

Elizabeth blinked. Unbelievable. What the heck did asking a guy out have to do with qualifying to beautify the school? Answer: nothing. Except in Jessica's twisted mind.

"Who? Whose name did you pick?" Elizabeth asked.

Robin dropped her hands and looked at Elizabeth, her bottom lip trembling. "Bruce Patman's!"

*Oh. My. God,* Elizabeth thought, feeling suddenly sick to her stomach. Bruce Patman. Of course. No one more untouchable. No one more evil. Even Jessica herself hadn't been able to hold his attention for long. If Elizabeth knew her sister at all, the box Robin had picked from had been full of slips with Bruce Patman's name on them and no one else's. It was a classic Jessica move.

"She may as well have told me to ask Elvis," Robin muttered.

Elizabeth couldn't believe it. How could Jessica do such a thing? She turned and looked toward the tennis courts, where Bruce and the team were, as they always were after school, practicing their game. Bruce, in his tennis whites, was on the nearest court, thwacking the yellow ball with incredible precision. Elizabeth knew that there were three things in life Bruce prided himself on: his Cadillac Roadster, his family name, and his tennis. He was the richest, hottest, most obnoxious guy in school, and if Robin asked him to the dance, he'd laugh right in her face. Or worse.

Unless . . .

Suddenly, Elizabeth was hit with an idea. There wasn't much in this world Bruce wanted, but Liz knew of one thing he was always whining about. One thing she had the power to give him. She was so exhilarated by the idea, she spoke before thinking it through.

"Robin, don't worry about it," Elizabeth said excitedly. "He's going to say yes."

"What? You're insane," Robin replied, stunned.

"I'm telling you," Elizabeth replied, jumping up. "All you have to do is get up the guts to ask him. Tomorrow. When you see him tomorrow, just walk up to him and ask him. I swear he'll say yes."

"No way," Robin said, shaking her head. "He thinks I'm a heifer. He tells me so on a daily basis."

*Jerk. Big fatheaded, moronic . . .*

"That's probably because he likes you and he's just . . . uh . . . covering!" Elizabeth said, improvising. "How could he not? Look at you! You're smart; you're pretty; you're funny. Just ask him, Robin. Positive thinking."

"But I–"

"Promise me you'll ask him," Elizabeth said, feeling almost manic. From the corner of her eye, she saw Bruce walk to the bench, towel off his face, and take a swig from his water bottle.

"Okay, fine. I promise," Robin said finally.

"Good. Now I've gotta go. I have something I have to do," Elizabeth said, backing away. "I'll see you tomorrow. And remember: Positive thinking!"

"Okay!" Robin called after her.

As Elizabeth rushed off to talk to the person she loathed most in the world, she started to wonder what she'd just gotten herself–and Robin–into. But no matter.

She was on a mission now–a mission to outwit Jessica Wakefield.

• • •

"Hey, Bruce. I've got a proposition for you," Elizabeth said, leaning against the fence that surrounded the tennis courts.

Bruce squinted at her and smirked. "Jessica Wakefield. Like I'd give you another shot after that stunt you pulled."

Elizabeth smiled, recalling how Jessica had shoved Bruce into the fountain at Guido's Pizza in front of half the class on the night she'd caught him cheating. One of her sister's finer moments.

"Look again, Patman," she said, stepping forward.

The smirk fell right off his face and he turned away, grabbing his racket. "Oh, it's you," he said derisively. "What kind of proposition could *Liz* Wakefield have that I could possibly be interested in?"

Elizabeth slipped through the gate and joined him near the small set of bleachers next to the court. "Oh, I don't know. Aren't you the one who's always whining that the school Web site never gives the tennis team enough coverage?"

He glanced over his shoulder at her and she could tell he was intrigued. "I don't whine," he said. "But yeah. I mean, you do a profile on Matthews; you do a profile on Johnson. Where's the profile on the star of the tennis team?"

"And who would that be?" Elizabeth asked, arching her eyebrows.

Bruce scoffed. "Please," he said, opening his arms. "All-county first singles? Captain? Undefeated this season?"

"Interesting," Elizabeth said with a thoughtful nod. "Maybe I'll run it by Penny. I think maybe you do deserve a feature."

"You got that right," Bruce said cockily.

"But if I do that for you, what are you going to do for me?" Elizabeth mused.

Bruce looked her up and down and turned to her fully for the first time, a mischievous glint in his blue eyes. "I thought you were with Wilkins. But okay. What did you have in mind?" he asked, sidling closer to her.

*Ew. No,* Elizabeth thought, gagging.

"Actually, I am with Wilkins," she replied wryly. "But there is something you could do for me. In good faith. And, you know, on the DL."

"What's that?" he asked, still flirtatious.

"I heard Robin Wilson is going to ask you to the seventies dance. I want you to go with her," Elizabeth said.

Bruce looked stunned for a split second, and then he cracked up laughing so hard he doubled over.

"The Wilsonator? Are you kidding me?" he sputtered.

"I'm dead serious," Elizabeth said firmly.

"That's a good one. I had no idea you had such a sick sense of humor," Bruce said, gasping for breath. "There's no way I'd be caught dead at the dance with that cow and you know it. Why are you wasting my time?"

He turned around and started to stride toward the end of the court, still laughing. Elizabeth saw red.

"I heard you got rejected from Stanford early decision!" Elizabeth shouted after him. "Daddy must have been so proud!"

All the guys on the court stopped playing and gaped at either Bruce or Liz. Bruce stopped and turned, his face practically purple. He was in front of her in two strides.

"Who told you that?" he said under his breath.

"You dated my sister, remember?"

"That little–"

"You don't want to finish that sentence, Bruce," Elizabeth warned. "All I'm saying is, if a story were done about you–one, say, extolling all your many virtues"–she paused to swallow back bile–"and talking about how you're such an asset to the school and the community–that might go a long way toward padding your application so that the Stanford thing doesn't happen again. Especially if the local paper picked it up."

Bruce blinked as he took this in. "Do they do that?"

"Sometimes," Elizabeth said with a shrug. A little white lie. The *Sweet Valley News* had, so far, not picked up any of *her* stories, but they had repurposed some of Penny's and John's, so it wasn't entirely untrue. She turned and looked across the courts, where Tom McKay was putting the beat down on some poor freshman. "Or I could do the same story about Tom McKay. Aren't you both applying to Berkeley?"

She moved as if to go talk to Tom, and Bruce grabbed her arm. Score.

"Wait. Wait," Bruce said, gripping her so hard he was starting to leave marks on her skin. "All I have to do is take her to the dance?"

"That's all," Elizabeth replied.

Bruce took a deep breath and blew it out, looking up at the clear blue sky. "All right, fine. I'll take her. But you'd better play up how I whipped that guy at Palisades in our last match."

Elizabeth grinned. "It's a deal. And, Bruce, I think it's great how charitable you're being," she said facetiously.

"Shut up before you make me change my mind," Bruce replied. He turned toward the court and shouted, "McKay! You and me! Right now!"

Elizabeth felt bad for Tom as Bruce strode to the baseline, chasing the freshman off. She knew he was not happy about their little bargain, and she had a feeling that he was about to take it all out on his unsuspecting teammate. But she wasn't about to dwell on that now. She'd done it. She'd guaranteed that Robin would pass Jessica's latest test.

Which Wakefield was the better schemer now?

• • •

Elizabeth strode through the front door of her house on Calico Drive, feeling triumphant. It was kind of fun, pitting her wits against Jessica's. As long as she kept winning, of course.

"Hey, Liz!" Jessica called out, bouncing down the steps in her ice blue string bikini. With her slim body, she would never have to suffer the self-consciousness Robin had to live with on a daily basis. Elizabeth wished that Jessica would think about these things once in a while, but she knew it would never happen. Jess lived in her own little world. Everyone else was just visiting.

"Hey, Jess." She followed her sister into the kitchen, at the back of the house. "How's Robin doing?" she asked innocently.

Jessica placed one of her library books on the counter, snagged a bottle of raspberry iced tea from the fridge, and shook it up. "Oh, I don't know. She tries, but I kind of doubt she's going to make it."

"Why not? She's done everything you've asked," Elizabeth said, putting on a blank face. She toyed with the spine of Jessica's book–the one about making speeches that stick. Jessica was sure serious about winning the upcoming Miss SVH contest. Liz couldn't remember the last time the girl had taken books out of the library.

Jessica smiled slyly. "Well. So far."

Elizabeth dropped the book. She was loving every minute of this. Jessica had no idea that Elizabeth had already foiled her next plan.

"I don't know. I can't imagine what you could come up with that would stop her now," she said.

Jessica's smile widened. "Wanna bet?"

"Bet what?" Elizabeth asked.

"Two weeks' laundry!"

"You're on!" Elizabeth said. They shook on the bet and both of them laughed.

"You're going down, sucker," Jessica teased, grabbing her book.

"We'll see," Elizabeth replied.

With that, Jessica sauntered out the back door, placed her iced tea and reading material on one of the tables by the pool, and dove right into the water. When she surfaced a moment later, she was laughing triumphantly. Elizabeth rolled her eyes and headed for the stairs. Jessica had no idea who she was up against.

As Liz made her way through the foyer, the front door opened and in walked Lila Fowler.

"Oh, hi, Lila. Come right in," Elizabeth said sarcastically.

"Hi, Liz," Lila said, not picking up on her tone. "Is Jess here?"

"She's in the pool," Elizabeth replied. She was about to mount the stairs when she saw a sparkle on Lila's hand and she stopped in her tracks. "Wow, Lila! What a gorgeous ring!" she said, reaching for Lila's slim fingers. It was a massive pink stone flanked by an intricate filigree design. The kind of thing stars wore on the red carpet at the Oscars.

"Oh, thanks," Lila said with a shrug. She pushed her

Gucci sunglasses up into her hair and inspected the stone critically. "It's okay, I guess."

*Wow. Way to appreciate your bling,* Liz thought. *That ring could probably pay for this house.* She wondered if this diamond would be the next bauble to end up in her sister's jewelry box.

"Hey, Lila, how's your aunt?" Liz asked, curious about her mystery benefactor.

"What aunt?" Lila asked.

"The one from New York. The apparent shopping addict?" Elizabeth said.

Lila stared at her blankly. "Shopping addict?"

*Patience,* Elizabeth thought, gripping the banister.

"You know, the one who keeps sending you all the expensive gifts?"

Suddenly, something seemed to snap into place in Lila's mind. "Oh, right! Sorry. You threw me with the shopping-addict thing. Because the stuff she's sending me, she's not buying it. It's stuff from her personal collection."

Elizabeth narrowed her eyes. Something about Lila's rambling was off. She was usually as cool as a Popsicle. Liz had never seen her nervous in her life.

"Really? That's sort of–"

"You know, Liz, I'd kind of like to get out to the pool

before I lose all the sun," Lila said, turning on her heel. "I'll see you."

"Right. See you," Elizabeth said.

*So . . . that was weird,* she thought as she watched Lila stride through the kitchen and out the glass slider. *Why do I get the feeling there is no aunt in New York?*

And if there wasn't, then where was Jessica getting all those crazy-expensive pieces of jewelry?

# CHAPTER 5

TUESDAY CAME AND went with no mention of Robin and Bruce from any of the usual gossip hounds. On her way out of school, Elizabeth even passed Caroline Pearce, the most notorious bigmouth in school, and Caroline's largest piece of news was that one of the contestants in the upcoming Miss SVH contest had already been disqualified because of lewd content on her MySpace page.

Robin and Bruce–if it had happened–would definitely have been bigger news than that.

On her way to the Jeep, Liz found Robin's number in her cell phone and called.

Robin picked up on the first ring. "Hello?"

"Robin, it's Liz," Elizabeth said as she dug through her bag, looking for her keys.

"Oh, hi, Liz," Robin said meekly.

Elizabeth sighed. "You didn't ask him, did you?"

"Liz, come on! He's going to laugh in my face," Robin pleaded.

"No, he won't, Robin. I promise," Elizabeth replied. *He would have yesterday, I'm sure, but I've fixed all that.* "You have to ask him tomorrow. Think about it! Not only will you have the hottest guy in school as your date but you'll show Jessica you can take anything she can throw at you."

"I don't know, Liz. I'm not sure it's worth it," Robin said.

Elizabeth imagined the shock that would be on Jessica's face when she found out that Bruce had said yes to Robin. Nothing could be sweeter. "Believe me, Robin," she said with a sly smile. "It will be."

• • •

On Wednesday morning, Elizabeth spotted Robin in the hallway before homeroom and lifted her hand to wave. The second Robin saw her, she blanched and ducked into the nearest classroom. Clearly, she was still nervous about the Bruce thing. In fact, now that a couple of days had passed since Elizabeth and Bruce had made their deal, Elizabeth was starting to feel uncertain about it as well. What if Bruce decided to renege?

She turned around and made a beeline for the senior lockers. Bruce was checking his hair in his locker mirror. All about appearances, that one.

"Hey," Elizabeth said, walking up to him. "Has she asked you yet?"

"Not yet," Bruce said, shooting her an annoyed look. "Is this some kind of joke?"

"No. I swear, she'll ask you today," Elizabeth replied. *I hope.*

Bruce rolled his eyes and slammed his locker door. "Fine. Whatever. You got that story done?"

"It's already in the queue at The Oracle," Liz said. "All I have to do is file it, which I'll do as soon as I see you and Robin at the dance together."

Bruce smirked and started down the hall backward, his arms out at his sides. "Just waiting for the lovely lady to ask me," he said.

Elizabeth shook her head and started toward class. At least he hadn't backed out. Now all she had to do was pray that Robin would have a brave moment today. Otherwise, she was going to be neck deep in Jessica's laundry for the next two weeks. Not to mention her gloating.

• • •

Elizabeth was reading over her article about Bruce on Wednesday afternoon in the Oracle office, wondering if stretching the truth about SVH's number one jackass would permanently mar her journalistic integrity, when the door opened and slammed. She whirled around and found Robin bearing down on her, breathless.

"Omigod! Liz!" she said, hand to her chest.

"Robin!" Elizabeth stood up as everyone else in the office stared. "What's wrong?"

"Absolutely nothing!" Robin announced with a grin.

Elizabeth's heart skipped in her chest. "Omigod! He said yes!"

"Yes!" Robin cheered.

"Yay! Robin! I'm so happy for you!" Elizabeth trilled, hugging her friend. Bruce had really come through. Elizabeth could hardly believe it.

"I have to go!" Robin announced, backing up. "I gotta go shopping for a seventies outfit! Wish me luck!"

"Good luck!" Elizabeth called after her.

With that, Robin raced into the hallway, in complete bliss.

"What was that all about?" Penny asked, joining Liz.

"Robin Wilson is going to the seventies dance with Bruce Patman," Elizabeth replied loudly.

Half the room gasped and Elizabeth saw quite a few cell phones appear as if from nowhere. She grinned happily. It would take about ten minutes for the news to reach Jessica's phone. Maybe less.

"Wow," Penny said, looking out the door after Robin. "She could do so much better."

Elizabeth laughed and got back to work. She couldn't agree with Penny more. But for now, Bruce was serving his purpose.

• • •

Jessica trudged into the kitchen after cheerleading practice, dropped her pom-poms, book bag, and gym bag on the floor, and slumped down at the table. At the stove, Elizabeth was humming as she stirred a steaming pot of spaghetti sauce. Jessica could just guess what had her sister in such a happy mood.

"Bad day, Jess?" Elizabeth singsonged.

"So I guess that means you've heard," Jessica said, barely supporting her head with her hand. "How the heck did she get him to say yes? Did she threaten to sit on him?"

"Jessica!" Elizabeth scolded, sounding exactly like their mother. "You have to stop making jokes like that. It's just mean and it's beneath you."

"Whatever," Jessica said, rolling her eyes. "Besides, it's not just Robin. Coach Freeling announced that she's holding more tryouts for the squad next month."

"Why?" Elizabeth asked, tasting her sauce. "Are you guys not cheery enough?"

Jessica ignored the lame joke and slumped further. "She wants to compete in some regional thing in the spring and you need sixteen squad members. We only have twelve."

"Oh well. Maybe it'll be nice to get some new blood on the squad," Elizabeth said as she reached for the oregano.

"You don't get anything, Liz," Jessica grumbled. "We just got a team vibe going and now we're gonna have to break in four new girls! And you know I'm going to have to do most of the work. Doesn't anybody care about *me*?"

Elizabeth chuckled. "You obviously do. Sometimes I think you care about nothing else."

Jessica's skin flashed hot. She shoved herself up from the table and grabbed her things, suddenly energized. "I don't know why you even bother talking to me sometimes, Liz. Clearly you don't even like me."

With a sigh, Elizabeth put down her wooden spoon and turned to Jessica, her face full of condescension. "Well, lately you've been making it kind of hard with all this Robin stuff."

"So what? It's not like it even matters! She's going to the dance with him! It's like there's nothing she can't do!" Jessica wailed, desperate. "I mean, how did she get him to say yes? Seriously. Tell me. Because I do not understand!"

Elizabeth grinned. "Well, you'll have plenty of time to figure it out while you're doing my laundry," she said. "I left a basketful outside your room."

"Ugh!" Jessica groaned, beside herself. She turned and stormed out of the room, ignoring Elizabeth's laughter as it followed her up the stairs.

• • •

"Unbelievable," Todd said, smiling down at Elizabeth as they slow danced nice and close on Saturday night.

"What?" Elizabeth asked.

"You even look gorgeous in that ridiculous outfit," Todd told her, leaning down to kiss her lips.

Elizabeth laughed, her heart light and happy and perfectly in love. "I kind of like it," she told him, looking down at the colorful wrap dress her mother had dug out of one of the old trunks in the attic. She had found a pair of white platform boots at a consignment shop and then spent an hour feathering her hair. Way more time than she had ever spent on her tresses before, but totally worth it. She felt as if she'd stepped right off the set of *Charlie's Angels.*

Todd, meanwhile, was wearing black disco pants and a ridiculous paisley shirt open to the navel. Liz didn't even want to know where he'd found such things, because if they had belonged to his dad, that was a visual she did not want to dwell on.

"Are you going to do a little disco later? Shake those hips?" Elizabeth asked.

"If you're lucky," Todd replied, holding her even closer.

Just then, there was a commotion near the gym entrance. A few people giggled and Elizabeth turned to look. Robin had just walked in with Bruce striding next to her. He was dressed exactly like John Travolta in the classic disco movie *Saturday Night Fever*–white vest and pants, black shirt and all. And in a bizarre confluence of Travolta flicks, Robin looked exactly like Tracy Turnblad from *Hairspray.* Somewhere, she had found a full-on pink sequined tent dress, and while some people were laughing, Elizabeth thought she looked absolutely glam. Maybe it was more sixties than seventies, but it was just disco enough to work.

Robin swept into the center of the room, grinning the whole way, as Jessica, Lila, and Cara watched stonily from the edge of the crowd. As the couple of the moment reached the middle of the dance floor, Elizabeth found she was flooded with relief. It was over. Bruce had kept his end of the bargain. Until that moment, she realized, she had never been entirely certain that he would go through with it. Now all she had to do was move that story about Bruce into the shared server at The Oracle and their deal would be complete. *Take that, Jessica Wakefield.*

A little circle around Bruce and Robin opened up as the slow song came to a close. It looked like Robin was the star of the night. And then it happened. There was a momentary lull as the songs switched, and Bruce's voice could be heard clearly as he stepped away from Robin, leaving her alone in the center of the dance floor.

"Well, that's it. I did my part!" he announced. "Anybody else wanna steer the pink *Titanic* around the dance floor tonight? 'Cuz I'm out!"

And with that, Bruce turned and strode from the gym.

# CHAPTER 6

ROBIN COULDN'T MOVE. Waves of humiliation washed over her. She felt as if she *were* the *Titanic*, broken and sinking into the cold, unforgiving ocean. This could not be happening. She had been so excited, had spent so much time finding the perfect dress, doing her hair and makeup. This was supposed to be her night, the night everyone woke up and saw her not just as chubby Robin Wilson but as one of the most popular girls in school–with one of the most popular guys on her arm.

And now they were all laughing at her.

Snapping out of her shock, Robin was suddenly hit with the overwhelming need to flee. She turned around and frantically pushed through the crowd, headed right for the door she had walked through feeling like she was on top of the world moments before. People were saying things to her, but she couldn't hear them. All she could think about was escape.

Elizabeth and Enid caught up to her just as she reached the door.

"Robin!"

"Not now, Liz! I have to go!" Robin wailed, tears spilling onto her cheeks.

All that mascara. All that blush. She was going to look like a horror show in about five seconds.

"Wait, Robin. Come with us first," Elizabeth said. She firmly grabbed Robin's hand and pulled her down the hall and into the girls' room. Enid scurried behind them in platform heels.

"I can't believe them! I don't know who I'm madder at! Bruce for pulling that crap or Jessica for thinking it up!" Elizabeth rambled the moment they were inside.

"Jessica! You think Jessica–" Robin couldn't finish the sentence. She was too choked up. Jessica was her friend. She would never have *told* Bruce to be so mean. No. She couldn't believe that. Bruce was mean all on his own. He didn't need anyone's help.

"No. I don't know," Elizabeth said quickly, handing Robin a paper towel. "I'm just talking. I'm so furious."

"What can I do?" Enid asked as Robin blew her nose.

"Make sure no one comes in here until we're ready to come out, okay?" Liz asked, her voice lowering to a more normal pitch.

"Got it," Enid said, whirling back out of the room.

"Oh my God. I'm such an idiot!" Robin cried, bracing her hands on the sides of a sink as she tried to catch her breath. "I can't believe I actually thought he wanted to go with me! I'm never going to be able to show my face in school again!"

Elizabeth grabbed a few more paper towels and held them out to her. "It's my fault," she said apologetically. "I convinced you to do it."

"It's not your fault," Robin said. She turned on the faucet and splashed some cold water onto her face. "I mean, I did it. And he said yes! Why did he say yes? If he wanted to humiliate me, he could have done it any day of the week!"

Robin sniffled and dried her face with the paper towels. Taking a deep breath, she turned around and leaned back against the sink. Outside, she could hear Enid arguing with some girls about going down the hall to the next bathroom. She felt so ashamed of herself she wanted to die.

"Of course he didn't want to go with me," she said, looking down at her dress. "Look at me. Why would someone who looks like Bruce Patman want to go out with someone who looks like me?"

"Robin, stop it," Elizabeth said.

"Stop what? It's the truth! He's the hottest guy in school and he's right! I'm a heifer! I'm the pink Titanic!" Robin wailed.

"Robin, if you would stop feeling sorry for yourself for five minutes, you would hear how ridiculous you sound!" Elizabeth said.

"Great! Thanks! Just what I needed. More insults," Robin sniffled.

"I'm not insulting you. I'm just telling you to open your eyes and see Bruce Patman for what he really is: a superficial jerk who has nothing going for him *other* than his looks," Elizabeth argued. "Which, by the way, are *not* all that great once you realize there's a demon behind them."

Robin garbled a laugh.

"Meanwhile, you have the looks and a whole lot more," Elizabeth told her.

Now Robin guffawed. "Liz, please."

Elizabeth took a paper towel and wet it, then dabbed under Robin's eyes and wiped her cheeks. Then she turned her around and made her look in the mirror.

"Look at you! Look how pretty you are," Elizabeth said.

Robin couldn't do it. She looked away. "Liz, you don't get it. I hate mirrors. I spend most of my life trying to avoid them. I've always been fat and ugly, but living here . . . I just feel fatter and uglier."

"Robin, come on," Elizabeth said.

"No, Liz. You don't have to lie to try to cheer me up. It's not like I don't know the truth," Robin said, grabbing her purse. "I don't know what I was thinking trying to join the Beauties when I'm the biggest beast in school."

She saw the pity in Elizabeth's eyes and turned toward the door. "I have to get out of here. I just want to go home, put on some sweats, and pretend this night never happened."

"Great," Elizabeth said sarcastically. "That'll really impress Jessica."

"You really think I'm going to go back in there after what happened?" Robin said, throwing up a hand. "Forget it. First thing tomorrow, I'm talking to my mom about transferring schools."

"You don't mean that," Elizabeth said.

"You have no idea how much I do," Robin replied firmly. She had, in fact, never felt so sure about anything in her life.

The door opened and Enid stuck her head in. "Hey. I can't hold them off much longer, you guys. Are we okay?"

"We're coming, Enid. Thanks," Liz said. Then she looked Robin in the eye. "Well, just so you know, I hope you don't transfer. Because I would really miss you."

Then she slid her fringed bag off the counter and slipped out of the room. Robin hesitated for a split second, touched. Maybe with Elizabeth and Enid by her side, she could face school on Monday. . . . But then she remembered Bruce's look. The laughter. The comments. And it was all just too much. She fled from the room, past the line of girls waiting to get inside, past Elizabeth and Enid, and ran out the front door of SVH, never to return again.

• • •

"What the hell is your problem, Patman?" Todd shouted, getting right in Bruce's face. "What do you get out of screwing with people like that?"

Elizabeth stopped in her tracks in the gym lobby. All at once, a few of Todd's friends gathered around him to back him up. Elizabeth didn't know what to do first–try to stop Todd from throwing down with Bruce and possibly getting expelled, or go after Robin. She turned around to find Enid and instead bumped right into Allen Walters, one of the photographers for the Oracle.

"Omigosh, Allen. I'm so sorry!" Elizabeth said, her heart pounding as the noise in the corner escalated.

"My fault," Allen said, blushing. "I'm always in the way."

Allen was one of the shyest guys in school, preferring hiding behind the camera lens to being in the spotlight himself. But he was also tall and boyishly cute, and right now he was there–which was all Elizabeth needed.

"Allen, can you do me a huge favor?" Elizabeth asked.

"Sure, Liz. What's up?" he replied.

"Robin just ran outside and I don't think she has a ride home," Elizabeth said. "I'm really worried about her. Can you go make sure she's okay?"

Allen looked toward the door nervously. "Me? Now?"

"Yes, please! I have to go stop Todd before he does something stupid," Elizabeth said. "Please?"

Allen blushed even more deeply. "Sure. Okay. I guess," he said. Hands in his pockets, he loped toward the door.

"You're gonna have to go faster than that!" Elizabeth said, giving him a little push.

Allen tripped through the door and started for the

parking lot. Elizabeth took a deep breath, wondering exactly how many fires she was going to have to put out tonight, and rushed to Todd's side before anyone could rearrange anyone else's face.

• • •

Robin was halfway across the parking lot before she realized that she didn't have a car and someone was chasing her.

"Robin! Hey, Robin! Wait up!"

She whirled around, having no idea what to expect. But the last person she ever would have thought she'd find bearing down on her was Allen Walters. The guy had barely spoken to her other than to ask to borrow a pen once during a chem test.

"Why are you chasing me?" she asked.

Allen stopped short. Robin could only imagine that she looked frightening in the dim lights around the lot with her face half made-up, half smeared.

"I guess I *was* chasing you, wasn't I?" he said with a laugh.

Robin blinked. What was this guy's deal? "Yeah, you were. Why?"

"Why?" he asked.

With her already frayed nerves, Robin was getting a tad frustrated. "Yes, Allen! Why were you chasing me?"

"Um, well." He looked over his shoulder toward the dance and touched the back of his head. "I just . . . Liz said you were . . . and I . . ."

He looked down at his feet, apparently unable to continue. Robin felt as if she were about to explode. Why was this happening to her? All she wanted to do was get out of here and never look back and she was being thwarted by this random nervous boy.

"Well, if that's all you've got, I gotta go," Robin said, yanking her cell from her bag. It was going to be awful to call her mother and tell her what had happened, but she saw no other way.

"I just thought you needed help!" Allen blurted out.

"Help? Help?" Robin said. "Did you not see what happened to me back there?"

"Well, I . . . uh . . ."

"I'm a total loser, Allen! I am going to be picked on for the rest of my life for that! How, exactly, can you help me? Huh?" Robin raged.

Allen looked at her, stunned. "I . . . I just–"

"I mean, this has to be the biggest joke of the night!" Robin ranted. God, it felt good to shout–to get all this negative energy off her chest. "The whole world is crumbling around me and who offers to help me? Allen Walters! A guy who can't even finish a sentence!"

Allen turned red and started to back away. "Sorry. I just . . . sorry. I thought . . . I'd better go. I'm really sorry, Robin."

He turned and walked away, head down, hands in his pockets, and suddenly it hit Robin like a bucket of ice water: she had just taken everything out on him. On innocent Allen Walters, who was only trying to see if she was okay, which was more than she could say for anyone else aside from Elizabeth and Enid. She was a total bitch.

"Wait! Allen! Wait!" Robin jogged to catch up with him. "I'm sorry. I shouldn't have yelled at you like that. I guess I'm kind of freaking out here."

"It's okay," Allen said matter-of-factly. "It's totally understandable."

"What are you doing here, anyway?" Robin asked, gesturing at the gym.

"Hey. I go to school here too, you know," he said, cracking a smile.

Robin blushed. It was a nice smile. "I know. I mean, I guess I never saw you as the dancing type."

Allen shrugged, sighed, and looked up at the stars.

"I didn't mean it like a bad thing," Robin said quickly,

clarifying. "I just . . . usually see you in the library or in the chem lab or something. I thought you were too . . . serious for this stuff."

Allen smirked. "Yeah, well, even I have to get out of the library once in a while. But I guess I should have gone to the movies instead. I'm not the best at group situations."

"Me neither, apparently," Robin said ruefully.

Allen chuckled. "No. Movies are definitely safer. Did you know there's a Tom Hanks retrospective at the Valley Cinema this month? There's a guy who always knows exactly what to say."

Robin laughed. "So does Reese Witherspoon. Maybe we should get scriptwriters. I hear there are a lot of them looking for work right now."

Allen laughed for real this time. It was the kind of laugh that made her feel giddy inside.

"Well, I guess I should go," Allen said out of nowhere.

"You're not going back in?" Robin asked.

Allen looked at the door to the gym lobby. "Nah. It's really not my thing." Then he looked her up and down and tilted his head. "I mean, unless you want to go with me."

"What?" Robin laughed. "You're kidding."

"Well, no one ever solved a problem by running away

from it," Allen said wisely. "That's something I read during my many hours in the library."

Robin giggled. "You're funny, Allen."

"Really? Who knew?" he replied. "So what do you say? One dance?"

With a gulp, Robin looked tremulously at the lights glowing behind the gym doors. Five minutes ago she would have said there was no way she could do this. But now . . . the idea of dancing with Allen was seriously appealing. And maybe Elizabeth had a point. Maybe she should let everyone see how strong she could be.

"Okay," she said, her voice cracking. "But since we both stink in crowds, maybe we should just stick to each other."

"Sounds like a plan," Allen responded.

Then he reached for her hand and Robin blushed again. His skin was warm, his hand strong, reassuring. Together, they walked back into the gym. Robin cringed against the noise and the lights. They were a sharp contrast to the peace of the parking lot.

"One dance?" she said nervously as people started to turn and stare.

"One dance," he replied firmly.

Together they walked to the dance floor, staying on the outskirts. Allen put his arms around Robin's waist and she looped hers around his neck. Luckily, it was a slow song, so all they had to do was hold on to each other and step back and forth. At first, Robin was too embarrassed to look at him. They barely knew each other and here they were hugging in front of the whole school. But the more she looked around, the more faces she saw gaping back at her, so instead, she focused on his eyes.

His clear, beautiful brown eyes.

He stepped on her foot once. She stepped on his twice. And finally, mercifully, the song was over.

"Well," Robin said, releasing him.

"Well," he replied.

They stood there awkwardly for a moment, not looking at each other.

"Can I drive you home?" Allen asked suddenly.

Robin smiled. "Sure."

As they walked out, Robin glanced up at Allen Walters again. He was taller than she had realized. And those brown eyes had incredible green flecks in them.

# CHAPTER 7

"I CANNOT BELIEVE you think it was my fault!" Jessica sputtered, yanking her silver top off over her head. She pulled on her oversized SVH Cheerleading T-shirt, then leaned toward her mirror to remove her fake eyelashes. "Since when do you think I can control anything Bruce Patman does? No one has ever been able to tell that guy what to do!"

Elizabeth, who had been standing in the middle of Jessica's room, indignant, blinked and looked away. Jessica felt a skitter of suspicion shoot through her.

"I never even thought he'd agree to go with her," she said slowly, eyeing her sister. "You wouldn't happen to have any idea why he did it, would you?"

Elizabeth refused to look at her. "No. How would I know?"

That was all it took. Jessica knew. She knew that somehow, someway, Liz had convinced Bruce to take Robin to the dance. This was unbelievable. Since when could good-goody Liz out-plot her?

"Well, whoever got him to say yes really didn't do her any favors in the end, huh?" Jessica said with a shrug. "I mean, if he hadn't taken her, then she wouldn't have been so publicly trashed, you know? Kind of sucks, really."

Elizabeth's cheeks turned pink and Jessica knew that her comment had hit home. She turned around, smiling to herself, and kicked off her platform sandals, then shimmied out of her tight black pants and dropped them onto the floor.

"Whatever. She's going to be fine," Elizabeth said.

Jessica faked a yawn. "Yeah. I'm sure she'll bounce right back," she said sarcastically. "I'm exhausted, Liz. Can you get the light on your way out?"

But Elizabeth didn't move. "You do realize you can't keep her out of the Beauties now? I mean, enough's enough."

Jessica climbed under her covers and stretched. "Well, she still needs to be approved by a two-thirds vote," she said. "You've seen the handbook. You know the rules."

By this time, Elizabeth was beet red. "Jess! Give it up already! What did she ever do to you?"

"Night, Liz!" Jessica trilled.

Then she pulled the covers over her head and simply waited for her sister to storm out of the room.

• • •

The next day, Elizabeth decided to take a solo trip to the mall and do a little window-shopping–maybe check out the sale at the Gap–and basically get away from her sister. Jessica, Lila, and Cara had set up camp by the pool before noon, and as much as Liz would have enjoyed a swim, the three of them would have made it unbearable. Instead, she settled for the comfortable air-conditioning of the Valley Mall and the innocuous light rock music that pumped through its speakers.

Strolling along the familiar promenade, Elizabeth told herself that Jessica was wrong. There was no way the Beauties would vote to keep Robin out at this point. Not *all* of Jessica's friends had been born without hearts. Some of them had to see how hard Robin had tried, how brave she was, how much she wanted it. They couldn't all vote to keep her out just because she was a little chunky.

She had just comforted herself with this thought when the window of a new shop made her pause. The gold sign above the door read "Lisette's," and underneath were the words "Authentic French Imports." Each piece of unique jewelry in the window was more exquisite than the last. Intrigued, Elizabeth wandered in. Why not? This trip was all about killing time.

There was only one other shopper inside the small space, and a middle-aged woman behind the counter was showing him a selection of rings. Elizabeth strolled alongside the glass counters, admiring beautifully crafted gold earrings, a gossamer pin, and intricate filigree bracelets. A stand on top of the counter displayed an array of colorful beaded necklaces. Elizabeth couldn't help reaching out to touch one, and the moment she did, she recognized it.

It was the same necklace Lila had given Jessica. The one that had come from her aunt in New York.

"Can I help you?"

Elizabeth turned to find that the gentleman customer was gone, and the saleslady was eyeing her warily.

"No, thanks. Just looking," Elizabeth said. "It's such a pretty necklace."

"Yes. It is," the woman said, then pursed her lips. "Would you like to try it on?"

"That's okay," Elizabeth said with a smile. "But . . . out of curiosity . . . how much is it?"

"Two hundred dollars," the woman said, stepping closer to Liz.

"Two hundred?" Elizabeth practically choked. *For beads?* she thought. She was sure that if she walked to the other end of the mall, she could replicate the necklace at Bead It Yourself, the jewelry-making shop where all the middle school kids had their birthday parties.

"Well, that line is exclusive to my store. You would have a hard time finding another like it anywhere else," the woman explained, her tone clipped. She was clearly losing patience but didn't want to be rude.

"Exclusive? Really?" Elizabeth asked. "But a friend of mine . . ."

She trailed off when something shifted in the woman's eyes. There was a sudden brightness in them, but not the good kind. It was a suspicious, hungry sort of brightness.

"Excuse me?" the woman said.

Elizabeth's mind was processing fast. If the necklace was exclusive to this store, and the store had only this location, then there was no way Lila's aunt in New York could have sent it to her. Unless she'd bought it on a trip out here, brought it home, then mailed it back, which was unlikely–especially considering this place was so new it still had a "Grand Opening" placard outside. So what had happened? Had Lila bought it, decided she didn't want it, and then given it to Jessica? Somehow, that seemed even more unlikely.

"Miss, have you seen a necklace like this before?" the woman asked. She was now standing directly across from Elizabeth.

"Oh . . . well . . . no. I don't think," Elizabeth stammered, her face warming. "I mean, maybe something *like* it."

In her nervousness, Elizabeth moved a little too suddenly and bumped a tray of gold earrings that had been left out. The jewelry skittered across the glass counter.

"Oh my gosh! I'm so sorry!" Elizabeth sputtered.

She anxiously scooped up some of the earrings and placed them back onto the tray. The woman snatched the rest of them and quickly rearranged them on the black velvet, matching up the pairs. As she did so, Elizabeth saw something else familiar locked inside the glass case. It was a large yellow stone with a gold filigree design on either side. Exactly like Lila's monster bling from the other day–just in a different color.

*Wow. Lila really likes this store,* Elizabeth thought.

The saleslady stepped out from behind the counter,

checking to see if any stray pieces of jewelry had fallen onto the floor.

"I'm sorry. I guess I'm a klutz today," Elizabeth said earnestly. "Maybe I should just–"

The woman held up a hand. "Please stay here, young lady, until I'm sure I have everything," she said. She crouched down and picked up a couple of earrings, then returned to her spot behind the counter.

"Is everything all right?" Elizabeth asked, taken aback.

The woman sighed. "Yes . . . yes, I think it is," she replied. "It seems all the pieces are accounted for." For some reason, she seemed loath to admit this.

"Excuse me, I'm sorry," Elizabeth said, her heart pounding. "Did you think I'd *taken* something?"

The woman eyed her shrewdly. "No. Of course not. I would never accuse a patron of shoplifting without proof," she said. "But you might be interested to know that we've recently installed a security system. Lifting items from this store is not going to be so easy from now on."

"Okay," Elizabeth said, both offended and confused. Why was the woman telling her this?

"So the shoplifter who has been working the mall–and my shop in particular–had better think twice before coming back," she added. "In fact, the necklace you were admiring had a twin, but unfortunately that was one of the items that was recently taken."

Suddenly, Elizabeth felt faint. She had no idea what to say, but the saleslady was looking at her expectantly. Why had she ever come into this stupid store?

"Really?" she said finally, her mind whirling. "I–"

"Who is this person you said you saw wearing a necklace like this one?" she asked, nodding toward the display.

"Oh, it was just this girl in school. I . . . I don't really know her," Elizabeth sputtered, backing up. "I don't even know her name, actually. But thanks! I, uh, should go! Good luck with your store!"

She almost knocked over an incoming customer on her way out and hightailed it straight to the exit of the mall.

*It's nothing. It's nothing,* she told herself as she headed for the Jeep. *Jessica would do a lot of things, but she wouldn't steal. It must just be a similar necklace. It's just a coincidence.*

Unfortunately, she knew from experience that when it came to Jessica, there was no such thing as a coincidence.

# CHAPTER 8

ELIZABETH HIT HER snooze button for the third time on Monday morning and stared at the ceiling. She couldn't remember the last time she'd procrastinated about getting out of bed this long, but she was just so tired. After staring at the clock half the night, stressing over what to do about Jessica, she still hadn't come to a solid conclusion. And now she was going to be out of it all day. Not good. Especially not on a Monday, when the teachers were all ready and raring to go.

*Just go in there and ask her right now,* she told herself, listening to the music pounding through the wall between her room and Jessica's. *Yeah. Ask her what? "Hey, Jess? Done any good shoplifting lately?"*

Elizabeth turned over onto her side, pulled a pillow in front of her face, and screamed. She was that frustrated. Jessica had done a lot of underhanded, dangerous, and semistupid things in her life, but would she really steal? Would Lila, when she had enough money to buy the entire mall?

*Okay . . . okay . . . how about the casual approach?* Elizabeth thought. *Hey, Jess. Pick up anything at the Valley Mall lately that you maybe forgot to pay for?*

Elizabeth groaned and tossed the pillow aside. That was it. She was going to tell her mom exactly what had happened at Lisette's and let her handle it. That was what parents were for, right? Handling their kids' idiotic mistakes?

Of course, Elizabeth didn't really want to be responsible for giving her mother an aneurysm–which was exactly what would happen if she heard the story.

"Hey, Liz! What do you think of this?" Jessica demanded, bursting into the room through their shared bathroom. Privacy meant nothing to Jessica, unless it was her own. "Are you still in bed?"

"What does it look like?" Elizabeth grumbled.

"Wow. I see you've taken your nasty pills this morning," Jessica said. She walked over to Elizabeth's full-length mirror and struck a pose. She was wearing a black jersey T-shirt dress with a V-neck and her new–perhaps stolen–beaded necklace. "Okay, do you think this dress shows off the necklace or is it too blah?"

Elizabeth stared at the necklace. In her mind's eye, she saw that unpleasant saleswoman's face and her certainty that the necklace had been stolen. What if someone happened to see it around Jessica's neck–someone who knew where it had come from? Sweet Valley was a small town. You never knew who you were going to bump into.

"Jess, about the necklace . . . ," she began, then faltered. She couldn't ask her. She just couldn't. And then the germ of an idea formed in her mind. "It's kind of unflattering. I mean, it makes your neck look really short."

"What?" Jessica cried, her hands flying to her neck.

"I mean, it's like you have no neck at all. Like a frog," Elizabeth added.

"Omigod! Liz! Why didn't you tell me this before?" Jessica took off the necklace and dropped the two-hundred-dollar piece of jewelry onto Liz's desk as if it were made of dirt. "Great. Now I have to change."

She started out of the room and Elizabeth's tension abated just a touch. She still hadn't figured out a way to solve the bigger problem, but at least she'd prevented her sister from wearing the stolen merchandise. Appealing to Jessica's vanity always worked.

"Hey, Jess, where are you holding the meeting this afternoon?" Elizabeth asked, swinging her legs over the side of her bed.

Jessica froze. "Meeting? What meeting?"

Elizabeth sighed. "The Beauties. I know you're voting on Robin today," she said. "Enid bumped into Suzanne Hanlon at Casa yesterday and they talked all about it."

Jessica rolled her eyes and Liz knew she was imagining different ways to skewer poor Suzanne.

"It's in room 215," Jessica said through her teeth.

"Oh, so you *weren't* going to tell me about it," Elizabeth said, walking past Jessica into the bathroom. "That's good to know. Nice to see you're going to be fair about all this."

"Well, I just figured I'd vote for you! Save you the trouble!" Jessica said innocently. "I mean, I *know* how you love to spend every waking second at The Oracle. I just figured you'd rather be there."

"Gee, Jess. Thanks ever so much for your thoughtfulness," Elizabeth said sarcastically as her sister breezed into her own room.

"You're welcome, Lizzie!" Jessica trilled.

And Elizabeth slammed the door right in her sister's bright-eyed face.

• • •

As Elizabeth had feared, she yawned and stammered her way through the day. She spaced out so badly in history class she answered a question about the Civil War using the names of the generals from the Revolutionary War. Her teacher, Mr. Fellows, had a good laugh about it with the class, and Elizabeth wanted to die. Or kill Jessica for doing this to her. One or the other.

At least, she was happy to note, Robin had shown up for school this morning and didn't look any worse for the wear. In fact, she had eaten lunch with Allen Walters under one of the trees outside the school. Maybe it was lucky that he had been the person Elizabeth had bumped into during her moment of crisis on Saturday night. Maybe something good would come out of that nightmare after all.

After the last bell rang, Elizabeth dragged herself to room 215 and met Enid outside the door.

"What do you think?" Liz asked her best friend. "Does Robin have the two-thirds?"

"I don't know," Enid said, biting her lip. "I know

Suzanne and Jenna are going to vote for her, but everyone else has been really vague. With you and me, that's only one-third."

Elizabeth sighed. "Well, we'll just have to hope that there are four more people in that room with a conscience."

They stood back as Cara, Lila, and Jessica strode by them. Not one of them said hello or even looked at Enid and Liz.

"Yeah. Good luck with that," Enid joked.

Elizabeth laughed, but her heart was filled with dread as she walked into the room and took a seat near the back with Enid. She couldn't believe how quiet and serious the atmosphere was among the members of the Beauties. Two weeks ago, this club hadn't even existed. Now they were taking the voting-in of a new member so seriously it was like the end of the world.

"All right, everyone, we all know why we're here," Jessica announced, standing at the front of the room. "Before we start our first project tomorrow–the flower planting in front of the school–we must decide on whether or not to add our new applicant, Robin Wilson, to our membership. Lila?"

Lila stood and walked around the room, handing out small slips of pink flowered paper.

"The process is simple," Jessica continued, lifting her chin. "If you want Robin in, simply write the word 'yes' on your paper. If you want her out, write the word 'no.' When you're done writing in your vote, come up and deposit them in this box."

Jessica produced a pink plastic box from inside her cheerleading duffel bag and placed it on the teacher's desk at the front of the room. Elizabeth wrote "YES" on her paper, underlined it three times, and folded the paper in half. She was the first person to deliver her vote. Jessica stared her down as she approached the front of the room.

"Thanks, Liz!" she said brightly.

"Yeah. Sure," Elizabeth replied.

Enid went up next, quickly followed by the rest of the members. Once everyone was seated again, Jessica lifted the box. "Cara? As secretary it's your responsibility to count the votes."

Elizabeth's heart skipped a beat as Cara rose from her desk. "No way!" she blurted out.

Every girl in the room turned to gape at her. Elizabeth's face burned. Apparently, another symptom of a sleepless night was speaking before she thought it through. Still, they couldn't have Cara count the vote. Everyone knew she was one of the big three trying to keep Robin out. She could easily cheat.

"I mean . . . shouldn't two of us count?" Elizabeth said, improvising. "Just to make sure it's accurate?"

"It's twelve votes," Cara said flatly. "I know I'm not the math genius you are, but I think I can handle it."

Everyone twittered and Elizabeth sunk in her seat. Cara walked to the front of the room and began removing the papers one by one, sorting them into piles. As she removed the last two votes, an unmistakable smirk was plastered to her face.

*No,* Elizabeth thought. *No . . . No . . . No . . .*

"We have seven yeses and five nos," Cara announced to the room. "Robin Wilson is out."

A couple of people gasped. "What? Who voted her out?" Suzanne asked. "After everything she went through–"

"Everyone, please!" Jessica called out, holding up her hands to silence the chatter. "We know it's tough, but the committee has voted and the vote stands. Robin Wilson will not be a member of the Beauties."

Elizabeth sat there, silently fuming, watching as her sister adopted a look of grim resignation as if she were disappointed in the group. As if there weren't a "NO" in that pile underlined as emphatically as Elizabeth's "YES" had been–but in Jessica's writing.

"I just want to go on record as saying this sucks,"

Elizabeth said, standing up. "Robin would have been a real asset to this committee. The five of you who voted against her should be ashamed of yourselves."

Dead silence. Jessica smirked. "Thanks for the life lesson, Liz. We're all really happy to be put in our place."

Elizabeth glared at her sister but didn't back down. Didn't sit. Didn't move. She was not going to be the first to blink.

"Now, don't forget, we'll be meeting in front of the school tomorrow afternoon at five p.m., after our other practices and clubs are done for the day," Jessica said, gathering the votes and dumping them into the trash. "Wear your work clothes, but remember to still look cute! You're representing the Beauties!"

The meeting broke up and everyone crowded for the door. Most of the girls were speculating about which five had voted Robin out, but it was obvious to Liz. Jessica, Lila, and Cara had been three of the votes, and the only two other girls who didn't seem surprised or upset were Lanie Lawrence and Marisa Jenkins–two of the snobbiest girls in school. What were they getting out of this? What, exactly, did crushing a nice girl like Robin do for them?

"Sorry, Liz. But you didn't have to be such a sore

loser," Jessica said as she shouldered her bags. "That little outburst was really embarrassing–for you, I mean."

Elizabeth ignored her comments. "When are you going to tell her?" she demanded, crossing her arms over her chest.

"Tell who what?" Jessica asked.

"Robin. You're going to have to tell her she didn't get in," Elizabeth said.

Jessica wrinkled her nose. "Can't you do it? I'm kind of busy."

"No way, Jessica," Elizabeth said, stepping in front of her sister to block her path. "You orchestrated this. It's your responsibility to tell her."

"Fine." Jessica rolled her eyes. "I'll tell her tonight. Now, will you get out of my way? I'm already late for practice."

"No problem," Elizabeth said, stepping aside. "Just tell me when and where and I'll come with you."

Jessica, now a couple of steps past Elizabeth, tipped her head back in a groan. "But you *just said* you wanted me to do it!" she wailed, turning around.

"I do. But I'm going to be there to make sure you don't shatter her in the process," Elizabeth told her.

"Shatter her? God. Who knew you could be so dramatic?" Jessica asked. "Fine. We'll call her together and set the place when I get home. If that's okay with you, of course."

Elizabeth nodded. "I just can't wait," she said flatly.

• • •

The moment Robin walked through the door of Casa del Sol, Elizabeth wished she were anywhere else on earth. Robin's expression was so excited, so hopeful it made Liz want to hurl.

"This is going to suck," she said under her breath.

Jessica, sitting across from Liz in the booth, turned around and waved Robin down. "It's not that big a deal, Liz," she said quietly as Robin hurried over. "It's just a club."

Elizabeth wanted to explode. "If it's *just a club,* then why did you have to be such a jerk about the whole thing?"

An angry look passed across Jessica's face, but she didn't have time to put her thoughts into words. Robin was already bouncing into the seat next to Elizabeth.

"Hi, guys! I ran right out the door the moment we hung up!" she bubbled, her face flushed. "I think I ran three stoplights on the way here."

Elizabeth glanced at Jessica, wishing her sister would

wake up and see what her news was going to do, but Jessica–as always–had only her own wants in mind. She cleared her throat and leaned forward, lacing her fingers together on the Formica table.

"Robin, I want you to know that no matter what, we are always going to be friends," she said.

Robin's face changed instantly. It was all Elizabeth could do not to pick up her fork and stab her sister's hand with it. Not that she would ever do that. She just had a writer's imagination.

"I'm sorry," Robin said. "What does that mean?"

"It means that just because you aren't going to be a member of the Sweet Valley High Beautification Committee, that doesn't mean we won't still hang out," Jessica said earnestly. "I mean, I may not have a lot of free time on my hands, but–"

"Wait a minute. Wait a minute." Robin put one hand flat on the table and Elizabeth noticed that it was shaking. "Are you saying they voted me out?"

Jessica winced. "Unfortunately, yes. It was close, though. Seven for, five against. It just wasn't two-thirds, so . . ."

"Seven to five! Seven to–" Robin said, her voice rising. "But I did everything you asked me to do! I ran laps in front of the entire school! I played beach volleyball! I was completely humiliated at the dance for you people! How could you . . . How could you . . ."

Elizabeth reached for Robin's hand, wanting to find some way to comfort her. She felt proud that Robin was finally letting her anger show after everything she'd taken over the past two weeks. But Robin whipped her hand away.

"Don't touch me!" she shouted, attracting the attention of everyone in the restaurant now. "You're liars! Both of you! I don't know how you live with yourselves! I don't even know why I ever wanted to be friends with either of you!"

"Robin–" Elizabeth said, dumbstruck.

"No. I don't want to hear it," Robin said, shoving herself out of the booth. "I don't care what you two think of me. I don't deserve this. You know, when I first moved here and you guys were so nice to me, I really thought you were different. I thought you liked me for me. But no. You're just like all the beautiful people at every school I've ever been to. All you care about are appearances! Well, you know what? You can take your precious Beauties and go to hell!"

Robin turned and stormed out of Casa del Sol, tears streaking down her now pale face. A few of the skater dudes in the corner applauded her speech, but she was already out the door. Jessica shot them a glare and they all shut up.

"Well. That was fun," Elizabeth said weakly.

"God. Talk about dramatic!" Jessica said. "Now I'm even more convinced we did the right thing. We can't have someone that unstable in the Beauties!"

Elizabeth gaped at her sister incredulously. As if Jessica hadn't thrown more public hissy fits than any other girl in the history of Sweet Valley High.

"What?" Jessica asked innocently.

"I'm out of here," Elizabeth said, dropping the Jeep keys onto the table. "Have the car. I'd rather walk home than hang out with you right now."

Then, ignoring Jessica's indignant protests, Elizabeth grabbed her things and bailed.

# CHAPTER 9

Elizabeth sat in the Oracle office on Tuesday afternoon, her fingers resting quietly on her keyboard. Every once in a while, she glanced at her phone, which was sitting on the desk next to the computer, to see if she'd missed a text or a call. But the phone was silent. Robin hadn't shown up at school today, and she hadn't responded to any of Elizabeth's many e-mails, voice mails, and texts. Every time Elizabeth thought about the look on Robin's face yesterday, the things she had said, her heart felt strained.

Where was she? Had she just played sick for the day, or had something happened to her?

*She wouldn't hurt herself over this, would she?* Elizabeth wondered, swallowing hard. *When it comes down to it, Jessica is right. It* is *just a club.*

But still, Robin had clearly taken it very seriously. She had thought that being a member of the Beauties meant being a member of the popular crowd–meant being accepted. And that was the world to her. So it was possible . . .

"That's my ace reporter! Look at those fingers fly!" Mr. Collins joked, coming up behind Elizabeth.

Liz's hands sprang back as if the keyboard had turned white-hot. She looked up at her faculty advisor and smiled apologetically. "Just have a lot on my mind," she said. "Sorry."

"Don't apologize," he said, leaning back against the empty chair next to hers. English teacher by day, Web site advisor by later in the day, Mr. Collins was one of the younger, handsomer, and more popular members of the SVH faculty. The sleeves of his white shirt were rolled up, his yellow tie was loosened, and his dark blond hair looked as if he'd just run his fingers through it this morning and come to school. Every girl at SVH had a crush on him, but only a lucky few, such as Elizabeth, knew how crush worthy he really was. Because he wasn't just handsome; he was also a very good listener.

"I'm just trying to figure out why people who have

everything–popularity, style, money, looks–why they would want to tear other people down," Elizabeth mused, leaning back in her chair.

"Tear them down?" Mr. Collins asked. "How, exactly?"

"Well, like . . . excluding them from a club or something," Elizabeth muttered. "What would they get out of it?"

"Ah. It's an age-old story. The tale of the haves and have-nots," Mr. Collins said with a sigh. "Why do you think they do it?"

"Well, the obvious answer is that it makes them feel more superior by leaving other people out," Elizabeth said. "But that's so lame. I mean, don't they know how good it makes you feel to help someone? It's so much better than hurting them."

"I guess they'd never know that if they never bothered to try," Mr. Collins said. "Some people are just brought up to look down on people and step on people, so they never get to learn firsthand how good it feels to pick people up."

"Well, that's just sad," Elizabeth said.

"Huh. Sounds like a good opinion piece for the site, don't you think?" Mr. Collins asked. "You want the op-ed page this week?"

"Really?" Elizabeth asked, suddenly excited.

"I'll tell Penny," Mr. Collins said as he pushed himself

away from the chair. "Now, get to work!" he ordered with a grin.

Just like that, Elizabeth's fingers flew over the keys. She had a lot to say on this subject. And all she could do was hope that Robin would have a chance to read it.

• • •

The Oracle Web site was updated every Wednesday, so the next morning, Elizabeth's op-ed piece was all over school. She raced to the computer lab during lunch to read it again, relishing her headline, "Snobs Abound at SVH," and her smiling picture next to it. Unfortunately, Robin wasn't in school again, so Liz took a minute to e-mail her the link along with a message.

> Robin,
> I know you're mad, but I really just want to know that you're okay. Please just e-mail me something.
> Love,
> Liz
> PS Check out this article on the Oracle. I hope it helps.

She sent her piece to the printer near the window—she always liked to have a hard copy of her work—and went over to retrieve it. At that moment, the door to the lab opened and slammed and the few people at the computers jumped. Elizabeth looked up to find Jessica bearing down on her with fire in her blue-green eyes.

"Gloating, are we?" she demanded. "All proud of your backstabbing little article?"

"Ladies, I will not have a scene in my lab," said Mr. Wilder, the computer administrator. He stood up behind his metal desk, smoothing down his *Lord of the Rings* tie.

"It's okay, Mr. Wilder," Elizabeth said. She plucked her article from the printer and knocked the pages against the desk to straighten them. "We're fine."

"Oh, we are so not fine!" Jessica shouted, coming around the table and getting right in Elizabeth's face. "How could you? Everybody in the entire state of California knows you're talking about me and the Beauties! You called your own sister a snob on the Internet! That is so wrong!"

"Well, if the designer shoes fit," Elizabeth said, sliding by her sister.

A few of the kids in the room laughed. Elizabeth smiled in triumph.

"We are not snobs!" Jessica protested. "We held a vote! It was all perfectly fair!"

"Uh-huh," Elizabeth said sarcastically. "So making her run laps at lunch, making her wear a two-piece to the beach, making her ask that jerk to the dance . . . that was all perfectly fair."

"Well, there has to be some kind of weeding-out process!" Jessica said, indignant.

"There wasn't one for you or Lila or Cara! There wasn't one for me!" Elizabeth replied, shouldering her messenger bag.

"Well, clearly *that* was a mistake," Jessica said haughtily.

Now she got the laugh. Score one for Jessica.

"Ladies, really," Mr. Wilder said with a sigh.

"Sorry. We're leaving," Elizabeth said, heading out. Jessica followed her.

"Listen, Liz," Jessica said as she closed the door on the lab. "This is just as much your fault as it is mine."

Out in the hall now, Elizabeth let out a squeak as she whirled on her sister. "How do you figure?"

"You're the one who got her past the beach test," Jessica reminded Elizabeth, lowering her voice now that they were in the conspicuously deserted hall. "You were the one who wrangled her that date with Bruce. If she'd only failed one of those tests, it never would have had to go to a vote. You got her hopes up!"

Elizabeth was dumbfounded. No one knew that she had bribed Bruce into taking Robin to the dance–a deal she'd never made good on, considering what had gone down. "How did you–"

"How did I know about Bruce?" Jessica asked, smiling. "Well, apparently he was a tad pissed off that you didn't come through with some article you promised to write. He told Cara all about it during gym this morning."

*I'm such an idiot,* Elizabeth thought. *I should have known he'd mouth off if I didn't file that stupid puff piece.*

"You've known Bruce your entire life, Liz," Jessica said pointedly. "Did you really think he was going to let everyone believe he actually wanted to be with Robin Wilson? How naïve can you be?"

*I'm not the one who dated him and followed him around like his own personal geisha for weeks,* Elizabeth thought. But even in the heat of battle, she wouldn't hurt her sister by saying it out loud.

"Whatever, Jess. What's done is done," she said. "Right now all I care about is Robin. She's been out of school for two days and she hasn't been answering any of my texts or e-mails or anything. What if something's really wrong?"

"Why would I care?" Jessica shot back, crossing her arms over her chest. "I'm just a selfish snob, remember?"

Then she turned on her heeled sandals and strode down the hall toward the cafeteria. Elizabeth suddenly felt exhausted, as if all she wanted to do was curl up on the cold linoleum floor and take a nap. But then her cell phone beeped. She yanked it out of her bag, her hands shaking, and checked the text message.

liz. am fine. stop emailing me. robin.

A huge lump settled in Elizabeth's throat. Robin really hated her. But at least she was all right. That was a small relief. She shoved her phone back into her bag and trudged off to the caf.

• • •

The rest of the week passed with no sign of Robin. Then, on Friday night, Elizabeth and Jessica went to Guido's to pick up a pizza for the family, and Liz ended up walking into the pizzeria alone while Jessica conducted a "crucial" gabfest with Lila on her cell outside. Elizabeth almost tripped herself when she saw Robin and her mother sitting in a booth together, poring over some papers.

"Oh my gosh! Robin! It's so good to see you!" Elizabeth said, rushing over.

Robin put her fork down next to her almost empty salad bowl and sat up straight, staring stonily out the window. Mrs. Wilson glanced up at Elizabeth, looking half apologetic, half annoyed. Clearly, she knew what had gone down and what role Robin felt Elizabeth had played.

"Robin, listen, I hope you know I voted for you," Elizabeth said. "And so did Enid and a lot of other people. It was just that stupid two-thirds rule–"

"It's okay, Liz," Robin said flatly. "I'm over it."

"Okay, well, that's good," Elizabeth said, though she hardly believed it. "Are you coming back to school on Monday?"

Robin glanced at her mother, a plea in her eyes. "Actually, Robin's decided to be homeschooled for a while," Mrs. Wilson said.

"Homeschooled?" Elizabeth asked.

"She's just taking a little break right now," Mrs. Wilson said, placing some money down on top of the check, which was already sitting on the table. "We both hope you'll respect the fact that she'd like some time to herself."

Elizabeth was so taken aback she had no idea what to say. Had the Beauties really driven Robin to drop out of school? This was even more serious than she'd thought. At that moment, the door was flung open and Jessica rushed in.

"Robin! It's so good to see you!" she gushed, scurrying over.

The sight of Jessica was like a gunshot to Robin. She shoved herself out of the booth and Elizabeth had just enough time to jump back before getting knocked over.

"Can we go now, Mom?" she asked, not looking at either of the Wakefields.

"Absolutely," her mother replied. She gathered up the papers on the table and cradled them in the crook of her arm. "Have a good weekend, girls," she said. Then she looped her free arm around Robin's shoulders and together they walked out of the restaurant.

"How rude," Jessica said. "She didn't even talk to me."

Elizabeth had to hide a smile behind her hand. "Yeah. Really rude. Come on, Jess. Let's go get the pizza."

• • •

Saturday afternoon, Elizabeth walked downstairs in her bathing suit with a towel and a paperback novel and headed for the pool. She paused momentarily when she saw Lila stretched out on one of the chaise lounges, sipping a lemonade and talking Jessica's ear off. Was this girl ever not here? Didn't she have her own Olympic-sized pool in her own massive backyard? Why did she always have to use the Wakefields' pool?

Taking a deep breath, Liz resolved not to let Lila get to her. This was her house. She was going to do whatever she wanted.

"So . . . yeah . . . I've already applied to all these boarding schools," Lila was saying as Elizabeth slid open the glass door. "Daddy really thinks I'll have a better shot at an Ivy if I graduate from a *real* school."

It was all Elizabeth could do to contain a laugh. One of glee that Lila might be moving three thousand miles away and of incredulousness that anyone thought that straight-C student Lila would be getting into an Ivy from the hallowed halls of any school.

"Really? Omigod. I can just imagine you on one of those classic Connecticut campuses, all decked out in Burberry plaid and Izod," Jessica said with a sigh.

"I know," Lila said. "Of course, I want to go to the Sorbonne in Paris, so my father's talking to some people he knows over there as well. We spend so much time talking about my future. It's like he's obsessed with seeing me succeed, I swear."

Elizabeth lowered herself onto the chair next to

Jessica's and leaned back with her book. Neither of the other girls acknowledged her, which was more than fine by Liz. She opened her book and started to read.

"Oh, look at that! I'd better go," Lila said suddenly, checking her watch. She got up and slipped her silky cover-up on over her black bikini, pushing her feet into her strappy black sandals. "Daddy's meeting me at the spa for our facials. I'll see you later, Jess."

"Bye, Lila. Have fun!" Jessica called after her.

"Bye, Lila!" Liz shouted, just for kicks.

Lila simply lifted a hand as she walked back into the house.

"Oh my God. She is *so* lucky!" Jessica trilled, leaning back and tilting her face toward the sun. "I mean, the Sorbonne? Boarding school? I would *kill* to go to boarding school back east. It's so glam."

"Yeah, until you're trudging through three feet of snow every day to get to class and you entirely lose your tan," Elizabeth said wryly.

"Right. Good point," Jessica said.

Elizabeth glanced over at her sister. She was wearing the diamond earrings Lila had supposedly given her. Just the sight of them made Elizabeth's blood run cold. She had to find out what was going on with all the gifting once and for all.

"Jess," she said, laying her book aside. "Has Lila given you any more random presents recently?"

"Actually, yeah. She gave me this bracelet this morning," Jessica said, lifting her arm. Elizabeth's stomach turned. It was one of the bracelets from the case at Lisette's. She was sure of it. "Pretty, right?"

"Totally," Elizabeth replied, her mouth dry.

Jessica's lips twisted into a smirk. "What's the matter, Liz? Jealous? Sorry Enid doesn't have a wealthy, giving aunt in New York. But maybe one of her relatives will send you something from Podunk, Illinois. A cow chip, maybe?"

She laughed as if her dumb joke was hilarious.

"Jess, I asked Lila about her aunt in New York and she didn't even know what I was talking about at first," Elizabeth said, swinging her legs over the side of the chaise. "I don't think there *is* an aunt."

Jessica pushed her sunglasses up into her wet hair. "Liz, *what* are you saying?"

"I'm saying . . . actually, I'm asking . . ." Elizabeth hesitated. "Did Lila really give you all that jewelry?"

"Of course she did!" Jessica replied, confused. "Where else would I have gotten it? This bracelet alone is worth like a hundred bucks!"

"Try five," Elizabeth muttered.

Jessica's eyes widened in shock. "What?"

"I saw that bracelet in this new store in the mall called Lisette's," Elizabeth said, standing up. This conversation was too intense for sitting. "It's a five-hundred-dollar bracelet, Jess. And I don't think it came from New York. I think it came from that store."

"I don't get it," Jessica said, holding the bracelet with her other hand and staring at it. "What do you mean? You mean Lila bought this? You think she bought me a five-hundred-dollar bracelet? Even she couldn't get away with that. Her dad *does* go over her credit card bills."

Elizabeth took a deep breath. Her sister had always been a good actress. There would be no way to know if all this was just a line unless she asked her point-blank.

"Jess, I have to ask you something and I don't want you to freak," Elizabeth said.

"What?" Jessica looked at her as if she couldn't quite process what was going on.

"Did you . . . I mean . . . you didn't . . ." She sat down again and leaned toward her sister, looking her right in the eye. "Tell me you didn't shoplift that stuff from Lisette's."

Jessica's jaw dropped so fast Elizabeth thought it might break off. "Liz! Are you kidding me? Why would you even ask me that?"

"It's just . . . the woman at the store said that a necklace–

your beaded necklace exactly–had been stolen. And I just–"

"So you think I took it?" Jessica blurted out, standing up so fast she nearly kneed Elizabeth in the face. "Omigod, I know you've been mad at me lately, but do you really think I'd do something like that?"

"No! No, I don't. I don't know. It's just . . . I had to ask," Elizabeth said miserably.

"Well, thanks for your trust, Liz," Jessica spat, grabbing her towel.

"I was just worried about you," Elizabeth pleaded.

"Yeah, well, now I'm worried about you," Jessica replied. "You're obviously totally losing it."

Then she turned on her heel and stormed into the house. Elizabeth blew out a sigh and leaned back in her chair. That had gone about as well as she'd expected. But the good news was she believed her sister. Jessica's surprise and indignation had been genuine.

So where, exactly, was all that expensive jewelry coming from?

• • •

Sunday afternoon, Elizabeth hit the mall once more in search of a birthday gift for Todd. She felt as if she'd been neglecting him lately, between the beautification committee (she still believed in what they were doing, though she avoided the fab five Robin vetoers like the plague), The Oracle, and all her schoolwork. She wanted to get him something really nice, and after noticing how scratched and scuffed his watch was from playing pickup basketball with his friends, she'd decided to buy him one of those indestructible sports watches. Once inside, she headed directly for the Nike store, near the center of the mall.

On her way back to the car, after making her purchase, Elizabeth couldn't help strolling by Lisette's. There was something almost magnetic about the place now, considering all the mystery surrounding it. She paused near the window, pretending to admire the sparkling rings on the black velvet but really looking through the window into the shop.

There was a different salesperson today–an older man who was helping a couple in the corner. The only other shopper was a young girl whose back was to Elizabeth as she checked out a few bracelets on a black tray. The girl was obviously slim and stylish, as evidenced by the skinny legs sticking out of her shorts and her expensive sandals, but she wore an ugly oversized vinyl jacket, like the kind Liz's father wore on the rare days it rained in the valley.

Suddenly, the girl's hand flicked out and Elizabeth saw her palm the bracelet closest to her and slip it right into one of the jacket's many pockets. Elizabeth's heart was in her throat. What should she do? Should she point the girl out? Get mall security? Scream? Her brain was still reeling as the girl turned and calmly began to stride out of the store. Elizabeth stopped breathing. Just as the girl stepped over the threshold, Liz quickly turned and hid her face in her shopping bag as if she were searching for something. She counted ten Mississippis before finally looking up again and watching the girl walk across the mall.

Lila Fowler–the wealthiest girl in school–had a completely serene look on her face as she walked away from the scene of her crime.

# CHAPTER 10

Without even thinking about what she was doing, Elizabeth found herself following Lila through the mall. It was just too surreal. It had to be a joke. A prank. Some kind of dare. Why would Lila "I Eat Gold for Breakfast" Fowler ever need to steal anything?

But Lila didn't stop to giggle with some daring friends or convene with a hidden-camera crew for a laugh. She simply waltzed right out one of the main exits of the mall, climbed into her Mercedes, and sped away. It wasn't until Lila's car was completely out of sight that Elizabeth was able to think again. And once her brain started working, it produced only one thought.

"This cannot be happening," she muttered to herself.

As if on autopilot, Elizabeth walked back to Lisette's. Maybe it was her reporter's instincts or just plain curiosity, but she had to see what was going on back there. When she arrived before the brightly lit windows, she saw both the elderly salesman and the woman who had been working during Elizabeth's last visit to the shop frantically searching the counters and floors. Clearly, the woman had been in the back office before and now the two of them had just discovered that something was missing.

What happened next seemed to play out in slow motion. The woman, who was crouched on the floor, checking under the counter, looked up and instantly spotted Elizabeth through the window. Her eyes widened, and Elizabeth's heart stopped.

"You! Hey, you!" the woman shouted.

And just like that, Elizabeth's flight instinct kicked in. She turned around and sprinted out of the mall as if her sneakers were on fire. It wasn't until she was back in the Jeep and halfway home that she realized how perfectly guilty her behavior must have seemed. Hovering outside the store. Running from the scene of the crime. There was no doubt about it: Lisette's now thought she was the shoplifter. Her! Goody-goody Liz Wakefield, as her sister liked to call her. Talk about being in the wrong place at the wrong time.

Taking a deep breath, Elizabeth tried to calm her nerves. She was just rounding the corner into her neighborhood when she saw two figures jogging up the street. One was a totally ripped guy in a tank top and sport shorts. The other was a girl in a full sweatsuit. It was at least eighty-five degrees out. No need for such bundling.

*Why would anyone . . . ?*

And then Elizabeth was upon the joggers and her heart skipped a beat. It was Robin. Liz had no idea who she was with, but Robin was jogging like a pro, matching him stride for stride, with a serious look of determination on her face and sweat pouring down her cheekbones. Who was the guy? And what was she doing? She was going to sweat herself to death working out like that.

Had everyone in Sweet Valley suddenly lost their minds?

• • •

By the time Elizabeth got home, her guilt was overwhelming. She couldn't believe that part of her had thought Jessica could steal all that jewelry. Her sister was a lot of things, but she wasn't a common criminal.

Of course, she never would have suspected that Lila Fowler could be one either. Lila's father gave her every little thing her evil heart desired. She could have easily bought that bracelet if she'd wanted to, and then just charmed her father into paying the credit card bill later. What was the point of risking arrest when you had an American Express black burning a hole in your Chloé bag?

Elizabeth shoved through the front door of her house and ran upstairs, taking the steps two at a time. She tossed Todd's watch onto her bed before running through the bathroom and bursting into Jessica's room. Her sister, lying on the floor, her iPod blasting in her ears, was working on her campaign signs for Miss SVH.

"God! And you say *I* never knock!" Jessica said, startled.

"Jess, I'm so sorry," Elizabeth said, dropping to the floor next to her sister to give her a squeeze. "I'm such an idiot."

Jessica instantly sat up, pulled the earbuds from her ears, and went on high alert. She could sense major drama from a mile away. "What's wrong?"

"Nothing. I just suck," Elizabeth said, toying with one of the many markers strewn across the floor. "I can't believe I suspected you. I feel horrible."

Suddenly, Jessica's face lit up with a triumphant smile. "I *told* you I didn't tell Bruce to embarrass Robin! How did you find out? Did you talk to the jerkface yourself?"

Elizabeth blinked. It took her a second to jump to Jessica's train of thought. But when she caught on, she was more than happy to have something to think about other than Lila.

"Speaking of Robin," she said, leaning back against the end of Jessica's unmade bed, "I just saw her jogging up Peach Street." No need to mention the marine-type guy she'd been with. Jessica would be way too focused on that detail.

"Really? Amazing. The hermit lives," Jessica said, adding some glitter to the poster in front of her.

"You haven't . . . I don't know . . . heard from her lately, have you?" Elizabeth asked.

"From Robin? Uh, no. She totally dropped off the face of the planet," Jessica said. "I mean, home-schooling? Really? Could you be any more freakish? The whole point of school is to hang out with your friends."

*Unless your so-called friends treat you like dirt,* Elizabeth thought.

"Although, actually, now that you mention it, Cara said she thought she saw Robin walking into Fitness Max the other day," Jessica said, sitting up straight again.

"We all figured Cara was just having one of her momentary lapses of sanity, but is it possible that Robin is actually, like, working out?"

Elizabeth shrugged. "Maybe."

It would certainly make sense. That guy she had been with on the road practically screamed "personal trainer." Interesting development. It would be so cool if Robin had decided to get herself healthy. But wouldn't it be easier if she had some friends to support her?

"I wish she would reply to my e-mails," Elizabeth mused. She had found over the last week that she missed Robin's company. Her energy, her happy outlook, her sense of humor. Somewhere in the midst of all the stupid Beauties insanity, Robin had become a real friend. Unfortunately, Robin didn't seem to feel the same way about her.

"Yeah, well, you did set her up for the humiliation of the century," Jessica said with a scoff. "Can you really blame the girl?"

Elizabeth stopped the comeback on her tongue. It was pointless to argue with Jessica about this now. She *had* played a role in what had happened, even if she had only been trying to undo Jessica's awful plans. And she really didn't feel like getting into a fight right now. She had something bigger to discuss.

"Jess, listen, if I ask you to do something–something

that's really important–would you do it, no questions asked?" Elizabeth said.

Jessica's eyebrows shot up. Now she seemed really intrigued. "Like what?"

"Like . . . stop hanging out with Lila for a while?" Elizabeth said, then braced for the nuclear explosion.

"What?" Jessica screeched. "Why?"

"Just . . . trust me. I think she might be going through a . . . a thing right now," Elizabeth said, improvising. "She might not be the safest person to be around."

"What kind of thing?" Jessica demanded. "And why would you know about it and not me? I'm her best friend!"

"I just . . . know, that's all," Elizabeth said, pushing herself off the floor. The time was coming for a quick getaway. "And you probably shouldn't accept any more gifts from her either."

Jessica dropped her glitter paint and gaped up at Elizabeth. "Liz. You cannot just tell me to stop hanging out with my best friend and not tell me why."

"I said no questions," Elizabeth reminded her.

"Yeah! But I didn't agree to it! Liz! What the heck is going on? Have you heard something? Is she really going to school back east? Omigod! Is that it? Is she going to drop me and leave me in this boring town all alone?"

"I have to go, Jess. Just trust me. Don't make plans

with her right now," Elizabeth said, backing out of the room.

*At least until I figure out what to do.*

• • •

A week passed and Jessica, miraculously, seemed to be heeding Elizabeth's warnings. Liz didn't see Jessica outside of school with Lila once. But maybe that was because Jessica was so insanely busy. Between heading up the Beauties, working out with the cheerleading squad, and campaigning for Miss SVH, Jessica was such a whirl of activity she was barely visible.

Elizabeth knew it was asking for a miracle, but as she drove home from school on Friday afternoon, she hoped that the whole Lila thing would just go away. The girl couldn't keep stealing forever, right? Sooner or later she would get bored or realize she had enough crap stuffing her jewelry box already and just move on to some other distraction. Preferably something legal.

This thought was beginning to comfort her when she saw a solitary figure jogging on the sidewalk ahead. Robin again, but this time she was alone. She was wearing the same baggy sweatpants topped with an oversized T-shirt. Elizabeth spotted an empty driveway a few paces ahead of Robin and pulled in, hanging the Jeep over the sidewalk to block Robin's path. Liz was more than ready to beg Robin to talk to her, but when Robin looked up and saw Elizabeth getting out of the car, she smiled.

"Hey, Liz," she said, pausing to jog in place. She put her fingers to her neck to check her pulse.

"Hi, Robin," Elizabeth said, surprised. "Sorry to interrupt. I just . . . I hadn't talked to you in so long . . ." She pushed her hands into the pockets of her shorts, feeling awkward.

"I know. I'm so sorry," Robin said between breaths. "I've been meaning to write you back. The more I think about it, the more I realize the whole thing wasn't your fault."

Elizabeth suddenly felt as light as air. "Thank you! Robin, I swear I was only trying to help."

"I know," Robin said, still jogging in place. "And I also know that I was just being stupid. I had it all wrong. The whole thing."

"What whole thing?" Elizabeth asked.

"Jessica . . . the Beauties . . . the whole thing," Robin said. "I don't need it. I don't need any of it."

"Wow," Elizabeth said, impressed. "Good for you, Robin."

"Thanks. But right now I really have to go. I have to do another two miles before dinner," Robin said.

"*Another* two miles?" Elizabeth asked. "How many have you done?"

"Three so far today," Robin replied. "I'll see you around, Liz."

Five miles? *Five miles?* Elizabeth had never run five miles in her life. She wasn't even sure that she *could* run five miles. As Liz tried to process this information, Robin jogged around the back of Elizabeth's car into the street, hopped onto the sidewalk on the other side, and kept running.

"Wait! Robin! Are you ever coming back to school?" Elizabeth shouted after her.

Robin simply lifted a hand in a wave and kept on running.

• • •

Back in the Jeep, Elizabeth was about to call Todd and tell him about the encounter–maybe ask him if *he'd* ever voluntarily run five miles–when her cell phone rang. She checked the number. It was Lila's cell, which Jessica had programmed into Liz's phone for those many, many emergency moments when she couldn't find her own.

Elizabeth's hands started to sweat as she gripped the

wheel with one and the phone with the other. Why was Lila calling her? She pulled into her driveway and flipped the phone open.

"Hello?"

"Liz! Oh, thank God! You have to come!"

"Lila? What's the matter?" Elizabeth asked.

"We're at the mall. And she's . . . Liz, oh my God. It's a nightmare."

"She who? Is it Jessica? What happened?" Elizabeth asked, heart in her throat.

"She got arrested," Lila said grimly. "For shoplifting."

# CHAPTER 11

RUSHING THROUGH THE mall toward the food court, Elizabeth tried to stay calm, but it was pointless. Her mind was crowded with a thousand unanswerable questions. Was Jessica shoplifting after all? Were she and Lila in it together? Had they made up the generous-New-York-aunt story to cover for each other? Elizabeth caught quite a few disturbed looks as she raced past Carl's Jr. and McDonald's and ducked into the hallway that led to the mall offices. She had often noticed the dark little hole in the wall but had never remotely thought she would need to enter it.

"Liz! Thank God!" Lila jumped up from a line of

plastic chairs set against the wall, clutching a tissue. Her eyes were wet with tears.

"Where's Jessica?" Elizabeth asked.

"They've got her in there," Lila said, pointing at a fogged-glass door marked "Mall Security."

" 'They'? Who's 'they'?" Elizabeth asked, flipping into crisis-control mode.

"The mall security people!" Lila replied impatiently.

"So they haven't called the actual police yet?" Elizabeth asked, relieved.

"No. I don't know. I haven't seen anything but rent-a-cops," Lila replied, sniffling.

"Okay. Okay." Elizabeth took a deep breath, trying not to think about how scared her sister must be on the other side of that door. "Tell me exactly what happened."

"Actually, can't you just ask Jess?" Lila said, grabbing her purse. "I kind of have to go. . . ."

Elizabeth grabbed Lila's delicate wrist. "You're not leaving," she said firmly. "This is your fault, Lila Fowler. You're going to stay here and tell me what's going on."

Lila's brown eyes widened in indignation. "My fault? I didn't know she was stealing things!"

Unbelievable. So both of them *were* in on it. How

could this be happening? "Lila, what did Jessica take?" she asked, feeling dizzy.

"I don't know. Nothing!" Lila wailed. "All we did was walk through the door of this store Lisette's and all of a sudden these two people just, like, pounced on her and dragged her up here."

"What? You mean she didn't even get near the counters?" Elizabeth asked, confused.

"No! They said they've been waiting for her to come back," Lila explained impatiently. "Apparently she stole some other stuff before and they wanted to grab her before she did it again."

The truth hit Elizabeth so hard she had to lean back against the wall to stay upright. She brought her shaking hand to her forehead to steady herself.

"Omigod. They thought she was me," she said quietly.

Why hadn't she warned Jessica to stay out of Lisette's? Of course the saleslady–who suspected Elizabeth already–would mistake Jessica for her. She had no idea there were two Wakefield girls walking around with the same face.

"You! You've been stealing stuff too?" Lila hissed.

"Oh, shut up, Lila!" Elizabeth blurted out, finally losing control. "This is all your fault! I know you're the one who's been stealing!"

Lila backed up a step, taking in a dramatic gasp. "What? Why would I steal? I can have anything I want. All I have to do is ask my father."

"Enough!" Elizabeth said through clenched teeth, her fury rising inside her. "I saw you, okay? I saw you steal that bracelet last weekend!"

For the first time, fear and doubt crossed through Lila's eyes.

"And I know you've been giving half the crap you steal to Jessica. The necklace, the earrings, that bangle bracelet . . . ," Elizabeth rambled. "How much did you take?"

"I . . . I . . ." And that was all it took. Lila Fowler finally crumbled, hiding her face in her hands as she wept. "Oh my God. I don't believe this. I didn't mean for this to happen!"

"Why did you do it, Lila?" Elizabeth asked. "It makes no sense."

"You think I don't know that?" Lila snapped, lifting her face. She straightened her purse strap on her shoulder with a jerking motion.

"You just said you can have anything you want," Elizabeth said. "That your dad can buy you anything."

"Yeah! But that's *all* he does!" Lila wailed, more tears spilling over. She quickly wiped beneath her eyes with her fingertips, then shoved her hands under her arms and looked away. "You guys are so lucky, you don't even know. Your dad is home, like, all the time. *And* your mom. My mother took off right after the divorce and I've barely seen her since. And my dad is never around. I can't even keep track of him anymore. He's either in New York or Paris or Tokyo or wherever. I don't even think he knows I exist."

Elizabeth blinked, confused. "But . . . but a week ago you were talking about all the plans you were making together. School back east, the Sorbonne . . ."

Lila laughed bitterly. "Lies, duh. Remember how I had the solo at the fall concert? He was in town that night, but he didn't even show. And I e-mailed him a picture of the squad last week and you know what he wrote back? 'I didn't know you were on color guard.' Seriously."

"Oh my God," Elizabeth said, appalled. She couldn't imagine her father knowing so little about her life. "So is that why you've been stealing? For attention?"

It was so textbook it was almost sad. But Lila looked so distraught that Elizabeth's heart went out to her. She supposed these things were textbook for a reason.

"I don't know, maybe," Lila said, sniffling. "But as soon as I saw Jessica getting carted off, I realized how stupid it was. He would kill me if he found out. You've gotta get us out of this, Liz."

Elizabeth shook her head. Why her? Why was it always her cleaning up other people's messes? "Lila, come on. This is serious. Do you really think I can just wave some magic wand and it'll all go away? They know someone's been taking things. Someone's going to have to own up to it."

"But I–"

"You have to tell them the truth, Lila," Elizabeth said firmly.

"No! They'll tell my father!" Lila said, shrinking back.

Elizabeth's eyes flashed. "So you're just going to let Jessica take the blame?"

Lila looked at the security door. "No . . . I . . . I mean, can't you get her out of there?"

"Not without you," Elizabeth said. "Now, let's go."

Reluctantly, Lila turned toward the door. Her hand reached for the handle, but then she turned around, whipping Elizabeth in the face with her hair. "You have to promise me one thing," she said, her eyes desperate.

"What?" Elizabeth said impatiently.

"Promise?" Lila asked.

"If I can."

"Please don't ever tell Jessica about this? Or anyone else at school? I would never live it down, Liz," Lila begged. "Please. I can trust you, right? You're, like, a good person and all that."

Elizabeth almost laughed. "I'll do what I can."

"Thanks," Lila said.

Then she turned around, lifted her chin, and strode through the door. The first thing Elizabeth heard were her sister's muffled sobs. Her heart felt as if it were tearing down the middle.

"Can I help you?" a large man behind an incongruently small desk asked. His standard gray mall-security uniform was nearly bursting at the seams.

"Yes. I'd like to see my sister and we have some things we need to straighten out," Elizabeth said, looking pointedly at Lila.

"Your sister," he said, glancing over his shoulder. "Well, I don't know if I can–"

Elizabeth's patience was already worn way too thin. This wasn't Alcatraz. It was mall security. "Jessica!" she shouted at the top of her lungs. "Jess!"

Instantly, the sobs stopped and Jessica sprinted through the open doorway of one of the four cubicles behind the desk. "Liz!"

Elizabeth rushed forward and hugged her tear-streaked

sister. Two female security guards came hoofing out after Jessica and the taller of the two grabbed Jessica's arm.

"No, you don't," the guard said.

"Let go of her before I have my father sue you for unnecessary force," Elizabeth said without even thinking. The guard, however, blanched and released Jessica's wrist.

"There's two of you?" the woman said.

"Well, this is new," said the other, who, by the size of her badge, was clearly in charge.

"Liz! They were so mean to me! All I did was walk into this store and they grabbed me," Jessica cried. "Look at my arms!"

Sure enough, there were angry red marks on Jessica's upper arms where the security guards had nabbed her.

"I hope you know," Elizabeth said angrily, "that our father is one of the best lawyers in Sweet Valley. You can't just assault someone with no proof they've done anything wrong!"

At that moment, the door behind them opened and the woman from Lisette's strolled in, a triumphant smirk on her face. She walked right past Lila–the person who had *actually* stolen from her–as if she weren't even there.

"I see you've caught my little shoplifter," she said, looking down her nose at Elizabeth.

"No. Not that one. This one," the taller security guard said, gesturing at Jessica.

The woman's jaw dropped as she looked from Elizabeth to Jessica and back again. "Perfect. You have a decoy. Who knew the operation was so elaborate!" she exclaimed.

"There's no operation!" Jessica wailed, throwing her hands up. "I didn't take anything! I've never even been in your stupid store before today!"

"She's telling the truth," Elizabeth said.

"No, she's not. I saw her in the store twice before today," the saleslady said with a sniff.

"Did you actually see her take anything?" one of the security guards asked.

For the first time, the saleslady seemed uncertain. "Well, no. But she was right outside the store when one of our finest bracelets was stolen and she ran when I tried to talk to her. And she was in once before that and she knocked over a whole tray of earrings."

"And a pair went missing?" the guard asked.

"Well, no . . . but I was standing right there," the woman protested. "She must have chickened out or–"

"That was me. Both times," Elizabeth said. "So you can let my sister go."

"Liz!" Jessica said with a gasp.

The security guards looked at the twins, baffled, clearly not sure what to do. Apparently, their mall-security handbooks didn't cover twin situations.

"I told you it was this one," the saleslady said, lifting her nose. "It's those shifty eyes."

"Please! I didn't take anything either!" Elizabeth replied. "You said yourself none of the earrings went missing that day. And when I ran last weekend, it was only because you looked like you were about to pounce on me! What was I supposed to do?"

"Okay, I've had just about enough of this," the saleslady snapped. "You're telling me that you didn't take anything and she didn't take anything, but *somebody* has made off with more than two thousand dollars' worth of jewelry in the past few weeks. It didn't just get up and walk off on its own!"

"Two thousand dollars?" Jessica repeated, looking faint.

"Look, I think I can explain what's going on," Elizabeth said calmly, glancing surreptitiously at Lila. "But you have to let my sister go. No one saw her do anything, right? So just . . . let her wait outside."

Jessica looked at the guards hopefully. Finally, the guard in charge nodded. "Fine. You can wait outside while we talk to your sister."

"Oh, thank you!" Jessica exclaimed, bending at the knee she was so excited. She turned and reached for Lila's hand. "Come on, Lila!"

"Actually, I . . . I'm going to stay," Lila said weakly. "I'll wait for Liz."

Jessica's brow knit, but she shrugged. "Whatever. I'm out of here. I'll meet you guys at Jamba Juice! I'm *dying* of thirst after this!"

Just like that, she was gone. Apparently, if she was at all curious about what Liz and Lila were up to, that curiosity was completely obliterated by her concern for herself.

As soon as the door was closed, a hefty silence fell over the room. Elizabeth looked at the two female guards, who crossed their arms over their chests in unison and waited. She looked at the saleslady, who seemed to be at the end of her rope. She looked at the male guard, who was taking a bite out of a powdered donut as he watched with interest. Finally, she looked at Lila, who was as pale as a sheet.

"Well?" the guard in charge said at last.

"Lila? Don't you have something to say here?" Elizabeth asked.

Lila swallowed hard, took a step forward, opened her mouth to speak–and then fainted to the floor.

# CHAPTER 12

An hour later, Lila had been revived, had confessed to everything through quiet tears–promising to give all the stolen merchandise back–and was now sitting next to Elizabeth outside one of the cubicles while her father negotiated inside.

"I can't believe he came," Lila said for the third time.

"Of course he came. He's your father," Elizabeth replied.

*And the mall is threatening to press charges. If he didn't come for that, I'd personally stand up and give him the Worst Father of the Year award myself,* she added silently. She wondered how Lila intended to get the necklace, the earrings, and the bracelet back from Jessica without telling Jess why she was taking them. And speaking of Jess, where in the world was she? Elizabeth had been sitting there forever. Was she still sucking down Jamba Juice in the mall somewhere? Wasn't she at all concerned for her sister and her best friend?

"Can you hear anything they're saying?" Lila asked, still toying with a crumpled tissue in her lap.

"No. But if there's anyone who can intimidate these people, it's your dad," Elizabeth joked. She was happy when Lila managed a short laugh of agreement. Her sister's friend had been looking so pale and miserable Liz was really starting to worry. As obnoxious and elitist as Lila had been in the past, today Elizabeth had seen her soft inner core. It seemed that everyone, even girls who grew up in mansions and were surrounded by servants, had their problems.

Suddenly, the voices in the cubicle grew louder, and Elizabeth sat up straight. "I think they're coming," she whispered.

Lila let out a choking sound and turned her eyes hopefully and fretfully to the doorway.

"Yes. Yes. I'll take care of it," Mr. Fowler said. "Absolutely. I'll make sure she's there. And again, I'm very sorry for any trouble my daughter has caused."

A moment later, Mr. Fowler emerged from the small office. He was an imposing figure in his perfectly cut blue suit, his shoulders square, his blond hair perfectly in place. Behind him crowded the two female security guards and the pinched-looking saleslady from Lisette's.

"Girls," Mr. Fowler said by way of greeting. "Lila, come on, honey. We're going home."

Elizabeth and Lila stood as one. Lila kept her eyes trained on the floor as her father wrapped his arm around her.

"Elizabeth, thank you for staying with her," Mr. Fowler said. "You're clearly a very good friend to my daughter."

Part of Elizabeth wanted to laugh, but it was a very remote part, considering the circumstances. Little did he know that Lila's actual "best friend" had bailed an hour ago to get a smoothie and had never bothered to return and see if everything was okay.

"It was no problem," Elizabeth replied.

"Well, I'm grateful. Is there anything I can do to repay you?" he asked.

Lila looked up at Liz, her eyes impossibly sad. Elizabeth's heart fluttered. Could she really say the words that had just popped into her mind? Why not? She had already threatened mall security with a lawsuit today. Game on.

"You could spend some more time with your daughter, sir," Elizabeth replied.

Lila's jaw dropped and Mr. Fowler's handsome face turned beet red.

"Well, I . . ." He cleared his throat and looked around, refolding his trench coat over his arm. Everyone from the security guards to Liz to Lila watched him expectantly. "Clearly, yes. That might be a good idea. Thank you, Miss Wakefield."

Then he took Lila's hand and walked her out, but not before Lila threw a grateful smile over her shoulder. Elizabeth was about to follow, but the three guards and the saleslady from Lisette's were still standing there—hovering.

"I can go now, right?" she said.

"Yes. Of course," the woman in charge said, then glanced pointedly at the saleslady.

"And please accept my apologies," the saleslady said hesitantly. "I realize now that accusing you and your sister was a mistake."

"Thank you," Elizabeth said with a smile, feeling vindicated. She picked up her purse and turned to go.

"Wait!" the head security guard called out. "Your dad's not still going to bring a lawsuit . . . is he?"

Elizabeth's grin widened. "Not to worry," she said in a comforting tone. "All is forgiven."

She waited to catch the relief on all their faces, then turned and strolled out, feeling even more powerful than the formidable George Fowler.

• • •

Elizabeth found Jessica sucking down a pink smoothie as she bounced up and down on her toes outside the window of Abercrombie & Fitch. Liz took a deep breath to steel herself for what she was sure would be a barrage of questions. Lila had made her promise that she wouldn't tell Jessica a thing, and she intended to keep that promise.

"Hey, Jess!" Elizabeth called out casually.

Jessica's aqua eyes were huge when she whirled around. "Lizzie! Where have you been? I've been here forever! Where's Lila?"

She gripped Elizabeth's arm and looked past her, still bouncing. Apparently, somebody had asked for a few too many boosts in her smoothie.

"She went home," Elizabeth responded. "Which is what we should do. I'm exhausted."

"Not me! I could shop for another hour!" Jessica exclaimed, showing Elizabeth a couple of small shopping bags she clutched in her free hand.

"Nice to know your conscience wasn't at all compromised by the fact that we were detained by the mall police for so long," Elizabeth said wryly.

"What? I had to do *something* to keep myself occupied!" Jessica replied loudly. She scurried after Elizabeth, who headed for the door. "So what happened? What took so long? Did they figure out who the real shoplifter was? They didn't think it was Lila, did they? I mean, why would she *ever* shoplift? She's worth, like, a kazillion dollars!"

Elizabeth shook her head at her sister's antics. Luckily, Jessica was so hyper she barely even seemed to notice that Elizabeth wasn't answering her questions.

"Omigod! Do you know who I saw while I was waiting for you?" Jessica asked, grabbing Elizabeth's arm again and jumping up and down. "Robin Wilson! Her hair was all wet like she just got out of the shower or something and she went into that hair salon over by Neiman's! Seriously! Like, who goes to a hair salon looking like a drowned rat? And she was wearing one of those huge tent dresses. Like, God! At least *try,* you know? That's an exclusive salon!"

"Really? Robin was here?" Elizabeth asked. *Guess she finished up that five-mile run,* she thought. "Did you talk to her?"

"Me? No! Not after the way she treated me the last time! Please! Who needs her? She's, like, so yesterday," Jessica said. Then her eyes lit up as they passed Forever 21. "Omigod! Pink jeans!"

And she rushed ahead, clutching her smoothie, oblivious to the shoppers who jumped aside to get out of her way. Elizabeth chuckled under her breath.

*Well, Lila, thanks to Jamba Juice, your secret's safe . . . for now.*

• • •

Saturday afternoon, Elizabeth and Todd lay back on a huge beach towel in the sand, soaking up some rays, holding hands between them.

"I missed you," Todd said, squeezing her fingers.

"I know. I'm sorry. I've been so busy lately," Elizabeth replied. She turned onto her side and kissed his cheek. "I missed you, too."

"So today you're all mine, right?" he said with a gorgeous grin.

"All," Elizabeth said, kissing his lips now. "Yours," she added with another kiss.

Todd reached up to pull her to him and at that moment her cell phone beeped. Elizabeth sighed. If there was one thing she couldn't ignore, it was a beeping phone. With a sister like Jessica running around, she never knew when it might be an emergency. "Sorry. Let me just check that."

"No problem," Todd said with a wry laugh.

Elizabeth reached into her rattan beach bag, past the dog-eared novel she was reading and into the side pocket for her phone. When she flipped the cell open, she was stunned to find that the text was from Robin.

> LIZ- HAVE A FAVOR 2 ASK. L8R THIS WEEK. JUST WANTED 2 CHK 2 MAKE SURE IT WUD B OK.

Elizabeth blinked. Interesting. What kind of favor required advance notice? She texted back.

> SURE. AS LONG AS IS NOT ILLEGAL. ☺

Robin's reply came instantly.

> DEF NOT! THNX. WILL B IN TOUCH.

"Well. That was cryptic," Elizabeth said.

"Jessica?" Todd asked, shielding his brown eyes from the sun.

"No. Robin," Elizabeth replied.

"Really? How is she?" Todd asked.

"Okay, I think." She shrugged and turned to him. "Now, where were we?"

Todd was just closing his eyes for a kiss when the phone rang.

"Ugh!" Elizabeth groaned. She was about to turn the thing off when she saw Lila's name on the caller ID. "I'm so sorry. I swear I'll turn it off after this."

Todd smirked. "I'm about two seconds from finding a new girlfriend."

"Ha-ha."

She opened the phone. "Hello?"

"Hi, Liz. It's Lila."

"What's up?" Elizabeth asked. She didn't want Todd to know who she was talking to. It would bring up way too many questions.

"Listen, I know this is going to sound really insane, and if you don't want to do it, I understand," Lila began. "But I don't know who else to call."

*Okay,* Elizabeth thought, growing wary.

"What is it?" she said, prompting her.

"After school? On Monday? My dad and I have to go to juvenile hall to talk to some judge about the whole . . . *thing,*" she said, lowering her voice. "And Daddy's lawyer suggested that it would be a really good idea if I had, like, a character witness with me. And since no one else knows about this but you . . ."

*A character witness?* Elizabeth thought. *Me? What am I going to say? That Lila is the most shallow, self-centered girl I know?*

"I don't know," Elizabeth said, hesitating.

"Please, Liz. There's no one else I can call," Lila said quickly. "All they're gonna do is ask you if you believe I'm sorry, which I totally am, and if you think I'm a risk to ever do it again, which I'm totally not."

Elizabeth stifled an amused smile. "Okay. Fine. I'll be there."

"Omigod. Thank you *so* much, Liz! Daddy's gonna pick us up around the corner from school at exactly three-thirty, okay? So that no one sees us?"

"Okay. See you then," Elizabeth said.

She hung up the phone and turned to Todd. Robin and Lila sure were keeping things interesting lately.

"Here. Let me see that," Todd said, grabbing her phone. He flipped it open, turned it off, then hid it under his pile of clothes. "There. That's much better."

Normally, Elizabeth would have protested, but as she cuddled in his warm arms, she couldn't help agreeing. No more drama today. Today was all about Todd.

• • •

Elizabeth sat in the back of the Fowlers' black limousine, feeling quite uncomfortable in the silence. Lila and her father sat across from her, each staring out an opposite window. Mr. Fowler's BlackBerry kept beeping and vibrating, but he left it in his briefcase, ignored. As they approached the tall stucco facade of the Sweet Valley Municipal Building, Lila let out a worried sigh.

"Don't worry, Lila. We're going to work this out," her father said, covering Lila's hand with his own. "Everything's going to be all right."

Lila smiled and the tension was broken. Her father was so confident that even Elizabeth was suddenly certain it would all work out.

They met Mr. Lattner, Mr. Fowler's lawyer–a short man with dark hair and dark eyes–outside the building, then went up to see the judge in her small chambers. The window behind her desk took up almost the entire wall and afforded a beautiful view of the courtyard behind the building. The judge, however, seemed as if she'd never turned to look out on the sunny grounds. Her skin was creamy white; her dark hair was pulled back in a no-nonsense bun; and she wore a plain black suit with a white shirt buttoned up to her chin. As she sat down at her desk and opened Lila's file, she tsk-tsked under her breath. Lila shot Liz an alarmed look. Liz wanted to be comforting in return but couldn't muster it. This woman clearly meant business.

"Shoplifting is a very serious offense," the judge began, folding her glasses and placing them on top of the file. "I hope everyone here realizes that."

"Of course we do, Your Honor," the lawyer began. "But considering that this is her first offense, and that the store was willing to agree to leniency, we submit that–"

The judge held up one small hand. "I'd like to hear from Miss Fowler," she said. "What do you have to say for yourself, young lady?"

Lila glanced at her father, who nodded encouragingly. "Just that I'm really sorry. I only did it . . . for attention," she said quietly, looking at Elizabeth. "And I know that's stupid. I do. I'll never do it again."

The judge nodded. "Very well, Miss Fowler." She lifted her glasses to check the file again, then glanced up at Elizabeth. "And you are Miss Wakefield?"

Elizabeth's heart skipped a beat. "Yes, ma'am."

"I know your father. Good man. Good lawyer," the judge said.

"Thank you," Elizabeth said, her face coloring.

"So, Miss Wakefield, what do you say? Should I believe Miss Fowler?" the judge asked. "Do you believe she's learned her lesson?"

"Oh, yes," Elizabeth said without hesitation. "Trust

me. She's not a criminal mastermind. She just . . . like she said . . . she just missed her father."

"I see," the judge replied, glancing reprovingly at Mr. Fowler now. He shifted in his seat and cleared his throat. "I understand that most of the pieces of jewelry have been returned, and that restitution has been made for the missing items?" she asked.

"Yes, Your Honor," Mr. Fowler said.

Huh. Apparently Jessica was going to get to keep her stolen jewelry. Lila really was adamant about keeping this a secret if she'd convinced her father to pay for the things.

"All right, then," the judge said with a sigh. "Miss Fowler, I believe you've been sufficiently scared away from a life of crime. That said, if you step one foot out of line in the next six months, I will hear about it and I will not be so happy the next time you see me."

Lila looked incredulous. This woman seemed anything but happy. "Okay," she said meekly.

"Six months' probation," the judge said, making a note in the file. She slapped it closed and handed it to her clerk in the corner. "Good day to you all."

"That's it?" Lila asked weakly.

For the first time, the judge cracked a small smile. "Yes, Miss Fowler. That's it."

Elizabeth had never felt as relieved as she did when she stepped out into the air-conditioned hallway. Lila grabbed her and hugged her hard.

"Thank you so much, Liz," she said.

"You're welcome. I'm just glad it's over," Elizabeth replied.

"Me too," Lila said, flipping her brown hair over her shoulder. "You have no idea. I think I got a couple of premature wrinkles," she said with a disgusted nose scrunch. "But nothing a little Botox won't fix."

Elizabeth laughed. Lila was back.

"What do you all say to a celebratory dinner at the Palomar House?" Mr. Fowler suggested, wrapping his arms around Elizabeth and Lila as his lawyer chatted with the clerk. "I believe they have some scampi with our names on it."

"The Palomar House?" Elizabeth said. The restaurant was one of the most exclusive in the valley. "I don't know if I'm dressed for that."

Mr. Fowler laughed heartily. "As long as you're with me, kid, you could walk in there in a clown costume and they wouldn't care."

Lila laughed as well.

"Okay. Then I'm in," Elizabeth replied. She couldn't believe she was going to eat at the Palomar House.

Jessica was going to be so jealous! Oh, except that she couldn't tell her sister about it. Oh well. She was just going to have to savor the experience on her own.

"I'll have Danny bring the car around," Mr. Fowler said, fishing out his phone.

Just then, Elizabeth's cell phone beeped. She slipped it from its designated pocket in her messenger bag and flipped it open. It was another text from Robin.

"Who is it? It's not Jessica, is it? Don't tell her where you are!" Lila hissed, assuming that everything was about her, as always.

"It's not her," Elizabeth said. She walked over to the opposite wall to read the text.

did cheerleading tryout sign-up sheet
go up 2day ???

Elizabeth's brow creased. Why on earth would Robin want to know about that? She texted back.

Yes. I think so. ???

Robin replied right away.

do u know when deadline is?

Okay. This was unexpected. Why would Robin want to know about signing up for cheerleading tryouts? Elizabeth glanced at Lila and tried to ask casually.

"Hey, Lila . . . do you have any idea when the deadline is to sign up for cheerleading tryouts?" she asked.

"Wednesday afternoon. Why?" Lila asked, narrowing her eyes. "Do you know someone who wants to try out? It's not Enid, is it?"

Yes. Lila was definitely back.

"No, it's just . . . Penny," Elizabeth said, improvising. "She wants to put an announcement up on the Oracle site."

"Oh. Okay," Lila said, clearly relieved. "It's Wednesday and the pre-tryout practices start Monday afternoon. Tryouts are Thursday and the new members are announced on Friday."

Amazing how forthcoming she was once she was sure Enid wasn't involved.

"Thanks," Elizabeth said, biting back a sarcastic comment. She texted the info to Robin. Robin's reply was, again, quick.

gr8. sign me up wed after 8th OK? don't want any1 2 kno.

Elizabeth nearly dropped her phone. Robin wanted to try out for the cheerleading squad? She was coming back to school? Jessica was going to freak. She texted back.

What? Seriously? CHEERLEADING???

have alwys wanted 2 try it! ☺ C U in hmrm monday!

Elizabeth leaned back against the wall, her mind overflowing with questions, but when she texted Robin back, there was no reply. Apparently Robin had told Elizabeth everything she wanted her to know. For now.

# CHAPTER 13

ELIZABETH SAT IN homeroom on Monday morning, tapping her pen against the side of her desk nonstop. Every time the door opened, her head snapped up, and every time it wasn't Robin walking through the door, her spirits sank. If the total lack of Robin-related gossip was any indication, Elizabeth was the only person at SVH who knew that Robin was returning to school today after nearly a month away—and she couldn't wait to see her friend.

"Liz, will you please stop? You're making me tense," Jessica snapped from the desk behind Elizabeth's. "What'd you do? Mainline Starbucks this morning?"

"You're one to talk after the Jamba Juice debacle," Elizabeth replied.

Jessica was about to retort when the door opened and her jaw dropped instead. Elizabeth turned around to find Robin Wilson walking through the door, at least fifteen pounds lighter, three times tanner, and a hundred times more stylish than she'd ever seen her before.

"Oh. My. God," Jessica said under her breath.

The entire room fell silent, but Robin simply walked over to their homeroom teacher as if nothing was amiss and handed her a slip from the office. Robin's jeans sat low on her hips and a flowy short-sleeved blouse revealed miraculously toned arms. Her dark hair had been cut into a layered bob, which framed the cheekbones Elizabeth had always known were hiding under all that heavy hair. Her makeup was flawless and she wore a pair of high-heeled sandals that Elizabeth happened to know Jessica had been coveting at the mall for the last month.

"Hi, Liz!" Robin sang as she snagged the desk next to Elizabeth's. "Miss me?"

"Hi, Robin," Elizabeth replied. "You look amazing."

Robin grinned, showing off newly whitened teeth. "Thanks. I've been working my butt off–literally–so thanks," she joked.

Elizabeth laughed as Jessica stood up slightly in her

seat to check out Robin's designer shoes. Robin glanced up at Jessica and her drool as if she were out of her mind.

"Uh, what's up, Jess?" Robin asked. "You look a little pale."

Jessica fell back into her chair and shrugged, looking away. "Nothing. Nice shoes."

"Thanks," Robin replied. "I remembered you pointing them out to me on our last trip to the mall together and I just had to go back and get them."

Jessica's face flushed and Elizabeth stifled a laugh. Nothing annoyed Jessica more than when someone in school got a piece of couture she wanted before she had a chance. Apparently, Robin was aware of this, because she was smiling triumphantly to herself as she organized her notebooks. Score one for Robin.

Gradually, the chatter in the room started up again, then quieted for the morning announcements. Elizabeth kept checking Robin out from the corner of her eye as the secretary read off club meeting times and details of next week's Miss Sweet Valley High contest. The girl had completely redone herself from head to toe. Pedicure, manicure, delicate jewelry, new clothes. Even her posture was better. Elizabeth was dying to know all the details of Robin's weight loss and new attitude, but that could wait until later, when prying ears weren't listening in on every word.

"And finally, those of you who signed up for cheerleading tryouts, the first pre-tryout practice will be held in the gymnasium today, immediately following eighth period. All current cheerleaders are also required to attend."

"Yee-freaking-haw," Jessica grumbled, still upset that her squad was being tampered with.

The bell rang and everyone gathered their things.

"Hey, Liz, want to meet up for lunch in the courtyard?" Robin asked, hugging her books.

"Sure. Enid and I will meet you by the back door," Elizabeth replied, happy to see that any residual resentment had been forgotten.

"And, Jess, I'll see *you* after school," Robin said with a grin.

"What? Sorry?" Jessica said, clearly caught off guard.

"At cheerleading practice," Robin replied. "Wait. You don't get a vote there, too, do you? Because I don't think I could go through another hazing experience."

She said this with a cheerful smile, but Elizabeth could hear the venom behind it, the tone that said that Robin knew exactly what had gone on with the Beauties, and that she wasn't going to take that kind of treatment anymore. The few people around them froze in their tracks. No one ever publicly called out Jessica Wakefield. Jessica herself was stunned.

"No," she said finally. "Coach makes all the decisions on squad members."

"Great! Then I'll see you later!"

And with that, Robin turned and strode out of the room with her head held high, every kid in class gaping after her.

• • •

Jessica, along with all the other members of the SVH cheerleading squad, was teaching the squad hopefuls a brief dance routine and cheer, which they would all perform at tryouts. She had her group of four sophomores and freshmen in the corner of the gym and tried her best to remain patient as she worked them slowly through the steps. It wasn't easy, though. All four of them were hopeless. If she'd felt like being at all charitable, she would have told them to go home now and save themselves all the trouble.

But Jessica was not in a charitable mood, largely because Robin Wilson was in the center of the gym, attracting all kinds of attention.

"Wow. She's really good," one of Jessica's charges said, pausing in the middle of the routine.

Jessica turned around to watch as Robin moved through the complicated dance steps. Who knew a girl that size could have rhythm? Cara, who was in charge of Robin's tryout group, even looked impressed.

"You know, stopping in the middle of the routine just because something distracts you is not going to get you on the squad," Jessica snapped at the freshman.

"Sorry," the girl replied, looking scared.

"Whatever. Go take a water break," Jessica said, waving them off.

She turned and walked casually over to Cara's side as Robin finished the routine. Everyone in the vicinity clapped and cheered for the girl, and she flushed pink, clearly pleased.

"Nice work, Robin!" Cara said, slapping her hands together. "You're a fast learner."

"Thanks," Robin said.

"Cara, can I talk to you for a second?" Jessica asked, slinging her arm around her friend's tiny shoulders.

Cara blanched. Clearly, she knew she'd just been snagged making nice with the wrong person.

"Take five, you guys," she said to the group. Then she allowed Jessica to steer her away toward the bleachers.

"Okay, what are you doing encouraging her?" Jessica asked.

Cara pulled away and crossed her arms over her chest. "I'm sorry, but she's the best in my group!" she whispered, glancing over at the girls, who were now on their way to the gym lobby. "She has, like, mad skills."

"Mad skills? Seriously? She's still huge," Jessica snapped.

"Yeah, but not like she was. Plus she's strong. She'd make a perfect base," Cara replied. "And she told coach she already lost almost twenty pounds and wants to lose another twenty to get to her goal weight. She's got, like, a trainer and this whole diet plan that her mom's nutritionist friend worked out for her. I think she's gonna do it."

"How do you know these things?" Jessica asked, irritated.

"I eavesdrop," Cara replied matter-of-factly. "Maybe we made a mistake, not letting her into the Beauties," Cara mused as Robin reappeared at the gym door.

Jessica saw red. "You say one more word, Cara, and I'm done talking to you."

Cara stared at Jessica as if she were spouting algebraic equations. "What's the big deal? She's a nice girl and she's clearly trying to, like, better herself. Besides, what did she ever do to you?"

"Ugh! You sound just like Liz! That's it. Don't talk to me for the rest of the day," Jessica said.

Then she turned and stormed back to her group of hopefuls, ready to put them through the wringer. What had Robin Wilson ever done to her? Well, she hadn't just gone away quietly like she was supposed to when Jessica had gotten her rejected from the Beauties. The girl just refused to cooperate. Robin had snubbed her at Guido's a few weeks back, had been mean to her this morning in homeroom, and had ignored Jessica for the rest of the day. Nobody treated Jessica Wakefield that way. And now the girl was invading her life. Hanging with her sister at lunch, trying out for her squad. She was everywhere, and she no longer even seemed to care whether Jessica liked her or not.

Jessica just didn't get it. And she didn't like it when people were so unpredictable. She didn't like it one bit.

• • •

Elizabeth smiled when Robin walked into homeroom wearing a red T-shirt and a white skirt on Friday morning–the same day that all the current cheerleaders wore their red and white SVH uniforms to school in honor of the football game that night. It was as if Robin was saying she already knew she had made the squad. Liz loved her confidence.

"Hey, Robin. Nice outifit," Elizabeth said as Robin took her seat.

"Thanks," Robin replied. "I like that sweater. Where'd you get it?"

"It's mine," Jessica said. "She borrowed it from me."

"Oh. Well, you have good taste," Robin said to Elizabeth, without even looking at Jessica.

Liz could practically feel the angry heat coming off her sister at being so ignored. This had been going on all week–Robin giving Jessica a taste of her own sour medicine–and Elizabeth was starting to wonder if Jessica had blackened a part of Robin's heart for good.

"Good morning, students. We have a few announcements." The secretary's voice boomed through the speaker in the wall. "First, since I know there are many anxious girls out there, the new members of the SVH varsity cheerleading squad are . . ."

Elizabeth's heart started to pound so hard it was as if *she* had tried out for the team. Robin sat up straight in her chair but continued to doodle in her notebook as if the outcome was no big deal to her.

"Amber Brandon," the secretary announced, "Jennifer Horace, Kimberly Johnson, and Robin Wilson."

Robin let out a shriek that betrayed her nonchalant demeanor. Everyone in the room laughed and a few people, Elizabeth included, started to applaud.

"I can't believe it! I can't believe I actually made the squad!" Robin gasped, looking at Elizabeth.

"Congratulations," Elizabeth replied warmly.

"Yeah. Congratulations, Robin," Jessica said, sounding, if not pleased, at least genuine.

"Thanks, Jess," Robin said, looking at Jessica for the first time in days. "I never would have even tried out if it weren't for you."

"Really?" Jessica asked, happily stunned. Finally, a kind word from Robin.

"Yeah. I mean, if you hadn't kept me out of the Beauties, I never would have been motivated to change my whole life and everything," Robin replied.

Jessica's expression darkened. "Robin, *I* didn't keep you out of the Beauties. I told you. There was a vote and–"

"I know, I know. Two-thirds majority and blah, blah, blah," Robin said, waving a hand. "We all know you didn't vote for me and my bet is you had five votes locked in from the second you wrote that ridiculous rule book."

Elizabeth guffawed, then quickly slapped her hand over her mouth when Jessica shot her a look of death.

"But really, I'm over it. It's good. Because if I had joined the Beauties, I never would have had time for my campaign," Robin rambled.

"Campaign? What campaign?" Jessica asked.

Instead of answering directly, Robin stood up and commanded the attention of everyone in the room.

"Hey, guys! I just want you to know that as of this moment, I'm officially running for Miss Sweet Valley High," Robin called out. "I hope you'll all consider voting for me, and please spread the word!"

# CHAPTER 14

"At least writing The Insider is going to be beyond easy this week," Elizabeth said to herself, sitting at her desk in her bedroom on Sunday afternoon.

Penny had given her the task of writing up profiles for all the Miss Sweet Valley High contestants over the weekend, and she was just finishing up the final graph–all about Robin Wilson. Robin seemed to be making all the news lately. Between her mysterious one-month absence, her new sense of style, her winning a spot on the cheerleading squad, and her throwing her hat into the race for Miss SVH, Robin could have had a full column about her alone.

Elizabeth saved her work and opened her e-mail. The moment she saw her inbox, her heart skipped a beat. There was a message from Louis Westman, the high-school-beat editor at the *Sweet Valley News.* Elizabeth had sent him a few story pitches last week but hadn't actually expected to hear back, mostly because she had been sending him story pitches for two years and she had never heard a word in reply. Was this it? Had he finally seen something he liked?

*Omigosh,* please *let it be an assignment!* Elizabeth thought. Her hands shaking, she clicked open the message.

> Dear Miss Wakefield,
> Just a note to let you know I have received your pitches. You have some interesting ideas. Unfortunately, none of them are right for our paper at this time. But keep trying. You're clearly a talented writer, and I know one day you'll hit on the right thing at the right time.
> Sincerely,
> Louis Westman
> Senior Editor
> The Sweet Valley News

Elizabeth's eyes stung. She sat back in her chair, stunned. Why had he written her back now if it was still a rejection? Didn't he realize that just seeing his name in her inbox would get her hopes up? And what did he mean by 'the right thing at the right time'? All her story ideas had been topical. She wasn't some moron pitching a story about iPods when they were so five years ago already. Everything had been au courant.

She was just about to delete the e-mail when her door was flung open and Jessica came barreling in.

"Liz, which dress do you think I should wear for the Miss SVH ceremony?" she asked, holding up a red strapless minidress and a swishy blue floor-length frock.

"Whichever. They're both good," Elizabeth said morosely.

Jessica's face creased in consternation. "That is so not helpful. What's the matter?" She glanced at the computer screen. "Omigod! That guy finally wrote you back? What'd he say?"

Elizabeth looked at her sister, shocked. "You know who Louis Westman is?"

"Yeah! That dude from the paper who you've been, like, stalking since freshman year. You only talk about it all the time," Jessica said.

"I didn't think you were paying attention," Elizabeth said, completely flabbergasted.

"Liz! Come on! If it's important to you, it's important to me!" Jessica said, clearly offended. The dresses dropped at her sides. "Well? Did he finally accept something?"

"Um, no," Elizabeth said, closing the browser.

"Jerk. Whatever. His loss," Jessica said.

Elizabeth was so touched she could have cried. Jessica actually listened to her sometimes. Who knew?

"Hey! What's that?" Jessica demanded, leaning toward the computer screen. She had, of course, been distracted by her own picture smiling out at her.

"Profiles of all the Miss SVH contestants," Elizabeth replied. "They're going up on the site tomorrow before the assembly."

During eighth period tomorrow, the entire school would gather in the auditorium to watch as the contestants made a brief speech, then answered randomly chosen interview questions. Then the students would have all week to vote, and the winner would be announced during halftime at the football game the following Saturday.

"And you're writing them? Sweet! Hope you talked me up and talked everyone else down," Jessica said, reaching over Elizabeth for the mouse so she could scroll around.

"Jess! Hello? Personal space!" Elizabeth said, ducking under Jessica's arm and rolling away in her chair.

Jessica didn't even notice. She simply moved closer to the screen now that there was more room for her to do so.

"Why is my paragraph so much shorter than all the others?" she demanded, her face growing red. "You barely even said anything about the Beauties!"

"I mentioned them," Elizabeth replied.

"Yeah. 'Jessica recently created the new Sweet Valley High service club, the SVH Beautification Committee,'" she read. "It says nothing about all the work we've done. Nothing about the flowers or the gym wall or anything!"

"Well, I didn't put in the specifics of anyone else's charity work," Elizabeth pointed out, sliding forward again. "Your paragraph is only shorter because you have fewer clubs and awards than the other contestants."

"So? Delete some of theirs!" Jessica demanded, reaching for the mouse again.

"Jessica!" Elizabeth snatched the mouse back. "Give me a break! You know I can't do that!"

"But I'm your sister!" Jessica cried.

"And I'm a journalist!" Elizabeth replied. "And besides, if I leave something out, the girls are going to notice and then Penny will just make me put it back in."

Jessica sighed, crossing her arms over her chest so

that her two hangers clicked together and the dresses on them bunched up. "You don't even want me to win."

"Sure I do," Elizabeth replied.

*Although it would be kind of fun if Robin took the crown.*

"Come on, Jess. Do you really think anyone's actually voting based on who made the honor roll the most times or who lettered in the most sports?" Elizabeth said, saving her piece again and standing up. "We all know Miss SVH is a popularity contest. And who's more popular than you?"

Jessica grinned, shifting attitude so fast it almost gave Elizabeth whiplash.

"True!" she trilled, holding the dresses up again. "I think I'll go with the red. More school spirity. Thanks, Liz!"

Then she skipped out of the room, looking satisfied, as if Elizabeth had actually helped her and as if she hadn't been petulant and murderous two seconds ago. Elizabeth sighed as Jessica's stereo blared to life. She glanced at the smiling faces on her computer again and paused.

Nope. No one had ever been more popular than Jessica Wakefield. But Robin had been getting a lot of buzz lately and Elizabeth knew that the less popular kids in school really appreciated Robin's rise to fame. Was it possible? Could Robin Wilson have a shot at Miss SVH?

• • •

Unsurprisingly, all eight of the hopefuls for Miss SVH were articulate and beautiful and poised as Chrome Dome Cooper–the balding SVH principal–questioned them onstage on Monday afternoon. But by the time it was over, Elizabeth couldn't help feeling that Robin had shone a bit more brightly than the other girls. Maybe it was her genuine smile, her funny answers, or her self-deprecating jokes, but Liz felt that Robin had endeared herself to the student body more than the other, more egotistical competitors. And she was sure that Robin had received more cheers.

For the rest of the week, eight ballot boxes were set up along the cafeteria wall, each with a contestant's picture posted above it. Each student was given a card with "Miss SVH" printed on it. All one had to do to vote was pop that card into one of the boxes. Monday afternoon, Jessica strode right into the cafeteria and dropped her card into her own box with a flourish, but Elizabeth held on to hers, trying to figure out what she should do.

Should she be loyal and vote for her sister? Or should she vote for the person whom she thought would best represent SVH?

After a week of watching Jessica prance around school, handing out buttons and cupcakes and flirting with every guy in sight, and after a week of watching Robin chat with new friends, work her butt off at cheer practice, and ace the hardest chem test Liz had ever taken, Liz finally cast her vote on Friday. But first, she made absolutely sure that no one was around to see when she slipped her card into Robin Wilson's ballot box.

• • •

Saturday's game between the SVH Gladiators and the Palisades High Pumas was billed as a grudge match. Not only had Palisades beaten the Gladiators last season thanks to a questionable call by an official, but both teams were coming into the game undefeated. Sportswriters from up and down the coast had hyped the game all week, so Gladiator Stadium was jam-packed Saturday afternoon, not to mention the press box, which had been built to accommodate the Oracle sportswriter and maybe two other people. Now the writers, cameramen, and photographers overflowed onto the hill on either side of the bleachers.

"This is total mayhem," Robin said to Elizabeth as they stood under the bleachers before the game. "I cannot believe there are this many people here for my first game on the squad. I know I'm going to fall flat on my face."

"You're gonna be great, Robin," Elizabeth said. "Trust me. And if you do flub one step, no one will notice. Everyone will be too hyped up on adrenaline to even catch it."

Robin grinned. Her hair was pulled back in a ponytail, but a few layers still framed her face. She looked like the perfect all-American cheerleader in her brand-new uniform.

"Thanks, Liz," she said. Then she blinked, looking past Elizabeth's shoulder. "Um, I think that weird guy wants to talk to you."

Elizabeth glanced around to find the infamous Louis Westman himself hovering a few feet away. Liz recognized him from the small photo the paper always ran next to his stories. He wore jeans, a blue shirt, and a darker blue tie and had a stuffed laptop bag weighing down one shoulder. When he caught Elizabeth's eye, he lifted a hand in greeting, looking absolutely frazzled.

"Should I come with?" Robin asked protectively.

Elizabeth laughed. "No. I know him. I'll be fine. Break a leg out there!"

"Gee, thanks!" Robin joked. "Maybe I will!"

Elizabeth rolled her eyes and walked over to Louis Westman.

"Are you Elizabeth Wakefield?" he asked. "Someone told me to look for the blond girl who looks just like another blond girl in a cheerleading uniform."

Elizabeth laughed. "Yep. That's me. It's nice to meet you, Mr. Westman."

"Louis, please," he said, offering his hand. "Listen, there's a lot going on here today. Between the game and the controversy and this Miss SVH contest thing . . . I could really use a little help."

Elizabeth's heart skipped a beat. "Seriously? Because I'm already covering the contest for The Oracle. Do you want me to do a story for the paper as well?"

Louis's face lit up. "That's exactly what I was hoping! I know it's not the type of hard-hitting piece you've pitched in the past, but you have no idea what a huge help it would be."

"Please! I'd be more than happy to take the assignment," Elizabeth said gleefully.

"Great. Well, you have my e-mail. Say . . . five hundred words by tonight? Seven o'clock?" Louis said.

"Not a problem. I'm on it," Elizabeth replied. "And thanks for the opportunity."

"Thanks for not giving up," Louis replied. "Well, I'd better go try to stake a claim in the press box. Talk to you soon."

"Absolutely," Elizabeth replied.

She grabbed Lila's pom-poms as the girl strolled by, and screeched into them happily.

"*What* was *that*?" Lila asked, scrunching her nose.

"Sorry," Elizabeth said with a grin. "I'm good now."

"I'm so glad," Lila said. She was about to walk away, but instead she paused. "By the way, I just wanted to say thanks, you know, for keeping everything a secret from Jessica. I can't believe you haven't blabbed."

"Well, I promised I wouldn't," Elizabeth replied.

Lila smiled slightly. "Jessica promises not to blab all the time and it always lasts five minutes or less."

Elizabeth laughed. "Well, in case you hadn't noticed, me and my sister are a tad different."

"For once, I'm really happy about that," Lila said earnestly. "Anyway, I'll see you."

"Yeah. Later," Elizabeth replied.

She watched Lila stroll away, wondering if things would be less cold between the two of them from now on. She supposed time would tell. For now, she had a job to do.

Elizabeth fished her digital recorder and notebook

out of her bag and got right to work interviewing SVH students about their votes. She was going to prove to Louis Westman once and for all that she was a writer worth hiring.

• • •

As soon as the halftime whistle blew, Jessica, Robin, and the other two Miss SVH hopefuls on the squad rushed to the bathroom to change into their dresses for the big announcement. In front of the mirror, as they primped, sprayed, and touched up their makeup, Jessica mistakenly elbowed Robin in the cheek.

"Oh! I'm *so* sorry!" Jessica gasped.

Robin smiled at Jessica in the mirror. "No problem."

"Great dress," she told Robin, her eyes flicking over the strapless black floor-length gown Robin had chosen. "Very slimming."

Robin's smile twisted into a smirk. "I like yours, too. But you do know the guys have all voted already, right?" she said, giving Jessica's cleavage a derisive once-over.

Jessica blushed but chose to ignore the comment. It wouldn't look good if the about-to-be-crowned Miss SVH got into a screaming fight with another contestant right before the announcement. Instead, she smoothed her hair, then checked her profile. Perfect. There was nothing wrong with showing off one's assets.

"Well, good luck, Robin!" she said brightly.

"You too!" Robin replied just as brightly.

Jessica slipped by her and walked out of the bathroom, then yanked down on the hem of her minidress.

"Cow," she said under her breath.

She shook her hair back and walked regally toward the field. Already the makeshift stage had been set up on the fifty yard line and the classic Corvette convertible that traditionally drove the winner around the track idled in front of the SVH stands. Jessica could see the crown sitting on a red velvet pillow on the stage, glinting in the sun, and her heart skipped a beat.

*I want to thank all of my friends . . .*, she thought, rehearsing as she walked toward the field.

Soon all the hopefuls were lined up near the edge of the bleachers, ready to be escorted to the stage by some of SVH's male stars, all of whom wore full suits to do the honors. Jessica rolled her eyes as Bruce Patman strolled toward her, smoothing his tie, and she turned her back to him. Like she would really let him escort her.

*Tell him you'd rather walk out alone,* Jessica told herself. *No! Tell him you'd rather walk out with Winston Egbert!*

She was just getting ready for the big rejection when Bruce walked right by her and stopped next to Robin.

"Hey," he said, his voice low and sexy.

"Hi . . ." Robin looked confused. As did everyone around them.

"Listen, I wanted to apologize for the dance," Bruce said quietly. "I don't know what I was thinking. I mean, look at you. You're . . . hot."

Robin snorted a laugh. Bruce laughed as well. Jessica wanted to hurl. She had never heard Bruce genuinely apologize for anything during the entire few weeks they had gone out. And he'd done plenty worth apologizing for.

"Let me make it up to you," Bruce said. "Can I escort you onto the field?"

"Sure," Robin said, slipping her arm through his. "Why not?"

"Okay, *that* is just so wrong," Lanie Lawrence whispered to Jessica.

"Just ignore them. They're both losers," Jessica whispered back.

She gladly took Tom McKay's arm when it was offered, trained her eyes straight ahead, and strolled out onto the field, ignoring the excited buzz of the crowd prompted by the sight of Bruce and Robin together again.

Soon Jessica found herself standing on the stage behind Mr. Cooper, who was giving some yawn-worthy speech about the tradition of Miss SVH and what an honor it was to wear the crown. It was all she could do to keep from jumping up, grabbing him by the lapels, and screaming at him to get on with it already. She was more than ready to wipe that self-satisfied smirk off the Wilsonator's face.

"And now for the results!" Mr. Cooper said finally.

A roar of excitement went up from the crowd, and Mr. Cooper waited a few minutes for it to die down. On the field, Allen Walters circled the stage, snapping photos of all the contestants. Jessica put on her brightest smile as the lens focused on her. Finally, the principal slipped a white envelope out of his inner pocket.

*This is it. This is my moment,* Jessica thought. She could not wait to get that crown on her head. It was so much bigger, so much more impressive than the homecoming crown she'd won. And they would look amazing sitting next to each other on the shelf behind her bed. . . .

"This was one of the closest contests ever held at Sweet Valley High," Principal Cooper said. "And all your contestants are to be congratulated for doing a great job!"

More applause, cheers, and whistles from the crowd.

"It is my pleasure to announce that the winner of this year's Miss Sweet Valley High title is . . ."

He tore open the envelope. Jessica shifted in her seat, getting ready to stand gracefully.

"Miss Robin Wilson!"

# CHAPTER 15

Elizabeth shrieked with delight as Robin jumped to her feet. The SVH stands went absolutely berserk as Robin stepped shakily forward to accept her crown, her sash, and her two dozen red roses. Allen crouched below her, snapping photo after photo as she laughed and waved at the stands. Elizabeth knew she should be recording the reactions of the crowd, the mood and the atmosphere, but for the moment she could not tear her eyes away from Robin's excited face.

*She won! She really won!*

"I just want to say thank you to everyone who voted for me," Robin said into the wireless microphone. "I guess this is proof that if you work hard enough, you really can accomplish anything."

Elizabeth, along with the rest of the crowd, applauded like mad. She was so proud of Robin. So proud she didn't even want to look at her sister and the major puss on her face right then.

"Liz! Get out there! Get your interviews!" John Pfeiffer urged her.

"Right!"

Snapped out of her trance, Elizabeth rushed forward just as Bruce escorted Robin down the stage stairs and over to the waiting Corvette. Both Allen and the photographer from the *News* chased them, fighting for the best shot. The Corvette's driver, a middle-aged man from the classic car shop, stepped out and held the door open for the new Miss SVH and her escort. But Robin hesitated. She lifted the microphone and spoke into it.

"Actually, I was thinking . . . ," Robin said, biting her lip. "If it's not too much trouble, Bruce, do you think I could maybe ride in your car?"

"The Caddy? Sure. You have good taste," Bruce said smugly. "I'll go get it."

Bruce turned and jogged from the track. Elizabeth looked at Robin quizzically as the crowd murmured in confusion. This was new.

"Robin, why Bruce's car? Why him of all people?" Elizabeth whispered.

Robin turned the microphone off. "Miss SVH wants what she wants," she replied slyly.

Elizabeth knew that Robin was up to something–she would never say such a thing in seriousness–but she had no idea what. Two minutes later, the roar of Bruce's car engine was heard throughout the stadium and the black roadster came speeding out onto the track, top down and ready to go.

Bruce got out, tossed the keys to the Corvette driver, who managed to catch them even through his confusion, and offered Robin his arm again. Robin turned the microphone back on and spoke into it.

"Actually, I already have an escort in mind," Robin said. "Allen Walters? Would you do me the honor?"

A communal gasp echoed throughout the stadium. Allen nearly dropped his camera.

"What? I . . . I . . . ," he stammered.

"Come on. There's no one else I'd rather do this with," Robin said, waving him forward.

Allen beamed. He stepped forward, staring at Robin as if in a trance, and handed his camera to Liz. "Guess I'm part of the story now. Do you mind?"

Elizabeth laughed. "Not at all."

Robin and Allen had climbed into Bruce's car and settled themselves atop the backseat before Bruce recovered from his shock.

"Wait a minute! You're not taking my car!" he growled, stepping forward.

But the driver was already behind the wheel and starting to pull away.

"Thanks, Bruce!" Robin said into the microphone. "This was very generous of you!"

The crowd laughed and whooped and cheered as Bruce turned the color of cooked lobster. He started to go after the slow-moving car, then stopped, hesitated, and cursed under his breath. Elizabeth knew that he was realizing he would look like a complete psycho if he chased his own auto with Miss SVH riding in the back. So instead, he hung back by the fence, moping, as his prized Caddy was taken away from him.

As the car moved in front of the stands, the whole place went wild. Robin and Allen waved as hundreds of people took their picture. Liz, however, focused Allen's lens on Bruce. She couldn't help it. She'd never seen him look so utterly defeated.

"Back off, Liz," Bruce snapped.

"Sorry," Liz said with a laugh. "How about an interview?" She held up her digital recorder. "How does it feel to be publicly humiliated in front of the entire school–to finally get what you deserve?"

Bruce shot her a look of death and stormed off the track, and Elizabeth caught his retreat on camera, already writing the blurb for The Insider in her mind.

*A certain local millionaire got a taste of his own medicine at the Palisades game . . .*

Finally, the Cadillac finished its trip around the stadium and Elizabeth snapped as many pictures as she could of Miss SVH and her grinning escort. It was amazing how much things could change in such a short time. All Robin Wilson had ever wanted was to be popular, but it seemed she had been going about it the wrong way. All she had to do was be confident, take care of herself, and treat the people around her the way they deserved to be treated, and here she was–the most popular girl in school.

As Robin leaned in to kiss Allen, perched on the backseat of Bruce Patman's car, the Sweet Valley High stands erupted in cheers and Elizabeth knew she was about to write the story of a lifetime.

DON'T MISS THE WAKEFIELD TWINS' CONTINUING STORY IN

TURN THE PAGE FOR A SCINTILLATING PREVIEW. . . .

# CHAPTER 1

"WHAT DO YOU think? I'm going for 'sophisticated celebutante.' "

Jessica Wakefield stood poised before the full-length mirror in her twin sister's bedroom, chin thrown back, her glossy blond hair tumbling over her bare shoulder.

Elizabeth glanced up from her computer, where she was working on her latest entry for her gossip blog, The Insider. She narrowed her blue-green eyes as she took in her sister's heavy makeup and not-so-heavy clothing. The pink minidress she was wearing was so light, in fact, it was barely even there.

"Sophisticated celebutante? As in those loser girls

who are always on the cover of *Us Weekly* for getting arrested or starting fights in clubs or acting like total sluts?" Elizabeth replied.

"Liz–" Jessica rolled her eyes.

"Because if that's what you're going for, you've nailed it," Elizabeth finished, typing another line into her computer. "There's no way Mom's letting you out of the house like that. And didn't she already forbid you to go to this stupid party anyway?"

Jessica inspected her outfit from another angle. "Well, what she doesn't know won't hurt her, right?"

Elizabeth sighed and sat back in her chair, crossing her arms over her plain navy blue T-shirt. "So, what's your plan this time? Hide that outfit under something that actually covers some skin until you get out the door? Lie about where you're going? Or are you just going to sneak out your window and twist your ankle falling from the eaves again?"

"God! You're such a prude," Jessica complained with a pout.

"Yeah, well, whatever your plan is for tomorrow, don't include me," Elizabeth said. She was so over her sister's antics. For the last sixteen years, Elizabeth had found herself covering for Jessica practically every other day, and as of that day, she was done. Done.

"I don't know what you're talking about," Jessica said with an innocent smile–the same dimple-cheeked smile Elizabeth had, though Elizabeth's never looked as fake. "I'm spending the day with Cara tomorrow."

"Right," Elizabeth said sarcastically, glancing at her notes. "Since when does Cara have ill-advised facial hair and drive a black Viper?"

Jessica giggled. "Omigod. Cara would die if she heard you say that! Did you know she's been waxing her lip since seventh grade?"

Elizabeth's eyebrows shot up. Interesting. One of the most popular girls in school with a hidden 'stache? That might be a good tidbit for The Insider. But of course, she'd never be so cruel as to reveal something that one of Jessica's friends had worked so hard to keep secret.

"Come on, Jess. There's no way you're going to be able to hide this from Mom and Dad," Elizabeth said. "You can hear his car coming from ten miles away. And honestly? I agree with them. Scott is way too old for you."

Elizabeth had first met Scott Daniels the past weekend when he'd come to pick Jessica up at Casa del Sol, where they'd been hanging out with all their friends. It wasn't just his age that bothered Elizabeth. It was the insipid "twice as nice" comment he'd made when Jessica had introduced them—as if Liz hadn't heard that one before. And the way he'd greeted their friends with an indifferent nod, checking the place out as if he was looking for someone better to talk to. Plus he kept spinning his keys around his finger and checking his T-Mobile for texts. It was as if he was already looking forward to his next stop or trying to find someplace cooler to be. Elizabeth was surprised that Jessica, who preferred to be the center of her date's attention at all times, wanted anything to do with the guy.

Except for one thing: Scott was drop-dead gorgeous, even with the scruffy blond stubble around his mouth. Tall and tan, with sun-kissed, shaggy dark blond hair and a smile that could melt a thousand hearts, he had made all the girls at Casa drool. Even Elizabeth had found him attractive—until he'd opened his mouth. Plus he was a junior at SVU and a member of Delta Epsilon Delta—supposedly the coolest fraternity on campus. Elizabeth couldn't care less about those things, but to Jessica, they were swoonworthy. She'd been head over heels for Scott since they'd met a few weeks before at the beach.

"Please. Could you sound any more like Mom?" Jessica asked, diving into Elizabeth's closet in search of a pair of shoes. "It's the fact that he's older that makes him so perfect," she shouted, her voice muffled as she tossed sandals and flats and sneakers–shoes that had been perfectly organized and stashed away–over her shoulder onto the floor of the bedroom at random. "No stupid, childish games. I am *so* over high school guys!"

Elizabeth rolled her eyes. If her sister thought *that* guy was more mature than the boys at SVH, the girl was totally blind. Liz was only four minutes older than her twin, but sometimes she felt it was more like four years.

Jessica had a talent for attracting trouble the way a magnet attracted metal. And more often than not, Liz was the one she turned to for help when she got in over her head. The problem was that no matter how much Elizabeth protested, Jessica knew that her sister would always end up helping her out. And she took advantage of that whenever she could.

*But not this time,* Elizabeth thought resolutely.

"This halter top would look so hot with my red skirt," Jessica said, flipping her hair off her face as she emerged from the closet. She held up a scrap of white eyelet fabric. "Can I borrow it?"

"Jess, that's a scarf."

"Yeah, but if you tie it like this, it's a halter top!" Jessica replied, quickly knotting the ends behind her back, over her strapless minidress.

"Uh, if you wear that around Scott, you might as well wear a sign on your forehead that says 'ready and willing,' " Elizabeth told her, hitting the Enter button to send her column to her printer so that she could read it over.

"There's nothing wrong with showing a little skin, Liz," Jessica said. "We're young. We're hot. Why not?"

Elizabeth tried not to gag.

"I mean, seriously, you're totally wasting your bod dressing the way you do," Jessica continued, pulling a pair of Elizabeth's sandals from the pile. "You should play it up more. You could so rock the sexy-librarian look. Now you just look like, you know, a librarian."

Elizabeth laughed as she got up to retrieve her column. "Well, if rocking the sexy-librarian look means attracting guys like Scott, no thanks."

Scott had invited her along to this party his fraternity was throwing on the lake, but she had no interest. She had, in fact, been relieved when her mother had vetoed the whole thing. Everyone had heard about Delta Epsilon Delta's parties, and while most people thought that kind of debauchery was cool, Elizabeth definitely did not. Earlier in the year a couple of girls from the SVH cheerleading squad had crashed the Delta house on the night of one of their raves and had quickly discovered that they were overdressed. The rave had a pajama party theme. All the guys had been in boxers and all the girls had been in nighties and all the furniture had been replaced with mattresses. Unsurprisingly, the whole thing had gotten seriously out of control, especially with all the beer that had been flowing.

A beach party at the lake in the middle of the day sounded innocent by comparison, but with the Delta crowd, anything was possible.

Published by Laurel-Leaf Books,
an imprint of Random House Children's Books,
A division of Random House, Inc., New York.
Originally published by Bantam Books in 1984.